"What a **my**

Vanessa spit the words out, struggling, to no real avail, against the hands that imprisoned her with such gentle effectiveness. "Get out, and don't ever come back!"

Even in the half darkness she saw the pain in Nick's eyes.

"It's true, isn't it?" Vanessa ventured to ask, looking at him with wide eyes.

Nick sighed and released her hands. He shoved splayed fingers through his rain-dampened hair. "Part of it. I did come home one night and find Jenna and Parker together."

Vanessa felt herself breaking apart inside. "And you swore revenge?"

"Hardly. I beat the hell out of him and left. He didn't tell you that part of the story, though, did he?"

"You lied to me," Vanessa accused. "You used me to get back at him!"

Also available from MIRA Books and
LINDA LAEL MILLER

STATE SECRETS
USED-TO-BE LOVERS
JUST KATE

Coming soon

DARING MOVES
MIXED MESSAGES

LINDA
LAEL
MILLER
Only
FOREVER

MIRA BOOKS

ISBN 1-55166-073-3

ONLY FOREVER

Copyright © 1989 by Linda Lael Miller.

MIRA and the star colophon are trademarks of MIRA Books.

Printed in U.S.A.

For Debbie Korrell,
beloved friend.
Remember that serenity is never
more than twelve steps away.

1

This particular strain of flu, Nick DeAngelo decided, had been brought to Earth by hostile aliens determined to wipe out the entire planet—starting, evidently, with an ex-jock who owned one of the best Italian restaurants in Seattle.

Sprawled on the hide-a-bed in the living room of his apartment, he plucked a handful of tissues from the box on the mattress beside him and crammed them against his face just in time to absorb an explosive sneeze. He was covered in mentholated rub from his nose to his belly button, and while his forehead was hot to the touch, the rest of him was racked with chills.

He wondered when Mike Wallace would burst through the door, wanting the story. It was time to alert the masses to impending doom.

Did you actually see these aliens, Mr. De-Angelo?

Call me Nick. Of course I didn't see them. They must have gotten me when I was sleeping.

The imaginary interview was interrupted by the jangling of the telephone, which, like the box of tissues, was in bed with Nick. Hoping for sympathy, he dug the receiver out from a tangle of musty flannel sheets and rasped out a hoarse hello.

"Still under the weather, huh?" The voice belonged to his younger sister, Gina, and it showed a marked lack of commiseration. "Listen, if I wasn't afraid of catching whatever it is you've got and missing my exams next week, I'd definitely come over and take care of you."

Nick sagged against the back of the sofa, one hand to his fevered forehead. "Your concern is touching, Gina," he coughed out.

"I could call Aunt Carlotta," Gina was quick to suggest. She was a bright kid, a psychology major at the University of Washington, and she knew which buttons to push. "I'm sure she'd love to move into your apartment and spend the next two weeks dragging you back from the threshold of death."

Nick thought of his aunt with affectionate dread. It was in her honor that he'd slathered himself with mentholated goo. "This is not your ordinary, run-of-the-mill flu, you know," he said.

Gina laughed. "I'll alert the science department at school—I'm sure they'll want to send a research team directly to your place."

Privately Nick considered that to be a viable idea, but he refrained from saying so, knowing it would only invite more callous mockery. "You have no heart," he accused.

There was a brief pause, followed by, "Is there anything I can get you, like groceries or books or something? I could leave the stuff in the hallway outside your door—"

"Or you could just drop it from a hovering helicopter," Nick ventured, insulted.

Gina gave a long-suffering sigh. "Why don't you call one of your girlfriends? You could have a whole harem over there, fluffing your pillows and giving you aspirin and heating up canned chicken soup."

"My 'girlfriends,' as you put it, are all either working or letting their answering machines do the talking. And chicken soup is only therapeutic if it's homemade." Nick paused to emit another volcanic sneeze. When he'd recovered, he said magnanimously, "Don't worry about me, Gina, just because I'm putting you through college and paying for your car, your clothes, your apartment and every bite of food that goes into your mouth. I'll be fine without . . . any help at all.''

"Oh, God," wailed Gina. "The guilt!"

Nick laughed. "Gotcha," he said, groping for the remote control that would turn on the TV. Maybe there was an old Stallone movie on— something bloody and macho.

Gina said a few soothing words and then hung up. It occurred to Nick that she was really going to stay away, really going to leave her own brother to face The Great Galactic Plague alone and unassisted.

There was, Nick decided, no human kindness left in the world. He flipped through the various movie channels, seeing nothing that caught his fancy, and was just about to shut the set off and try to focus his eyes on a book when he saw her for the first time.

She was a redhead with golden eyes, and the sight of her practically stopped his heartbeat. She was holding an urn that was suitable enough to be someone's final resting place, and there was a toll-free number superimposed over her chest.

With quick, prodding motions of his thumb, Nick used the control button on the remote to turn up the volume. "My name is Vanessa Lawrence," the vision told her viewing audience in a voice more soothing than all the chicken soup and mentholated rub in the world, ''and you're watching the Midas Network.'' She went on to extol the virtues of the hideous vase she was peddling, but Nick didn't hear a word.

He was too busy dredging up everything he knew about the Midas Network, a nationwide shopping channel based in Seattle. The enterprise was a new one, and one of his friends—an executive with the company—had urged him to invest because he was certain that telemarketing would prove to be the biggest hit with consumers since the tube itself.

Nick shoved one hand through his hair, causing it to stand on end in ridges that reeked of eucalyptus. Undoubtedly, he thought, he was experiencing some kind of dementia related to the virus that had been visited upon him.

Without taking his eyes away from the screen, he groped for the telephone and punched out the office number. His secretary, a middle-aged woman named Harriet, answered with a crisp, ''DeAngelo's. May I help you?''

''I hope so,'' wheezed Nick, who had just finished another bout of coughing.

''You don't need me, you need the paramedics,'' remarked the secretary.

"At last," Nick said. "Someone who understands and sympathizes. Harriet, find Paul Harmon's number for me, will you please? I'm in no condition to hunt all over for the phone book."

It was easy to picture Harriet, plump and efficient, flipping expertly through her Rolodex. "His office number is 555-9876," she said.

Nick found a pencil in the paraphernalia that had collected on the end table beside the hide-a-bed and wrote the digits on the corner of the tissue box, along with the home number Harriet gave him next.

The woman on the screen was now offering a set of bird figurines.

"Oh, lady," Nick said aloud as he waited for Paul Harmon to come on the line, "I want your body, I want your soul, I want you to have my baby."

The goddess smiled. "All this can be yours for only nineteen-ninety-five," she said.

"Sold," replied Nick.

Vanessa Lawrence inserted her cash card into the automatic teller machine in Quickee Food Mart and tapped one foot while she waited for the money to appear. A glance at her watch told her she was due at her lawyer's office in just ten minutes, and the drive downtown would take fifteen.

Her foot moved faster.

The machine made an alarming grinding noise, but no currency came out of the little slot, and Vanessa's card was still somewhere in the bowels of the gizmo. From the sound of things, it was being systematically digested.

Somewhat wildly, she began pushing buttons. The words *Your transaction is now completed*, were frozen on the small screen. She glanced back over one shoulder, hoping for help from the clerk, but everyone in the neighborhood seemed to be in the convenience store that afternoon, buying bread and milk.

"Damn!" she breathed, slamming her fist against the face of the machine.

A woman wearing pink foam rollers in her hair appeared at Vanessa's side. "You're on TV, aren't you?" she asked. "On that new shopping channel, the something-or-other station."

Vanessa smiled, even though it was the last thing she felt like doing. "The Midas Network," she said, before giving the machine another despairing look. "Just give me back my card," she told the apparatus, "and I won't make any trouble, I promise."

"I watch you every day," the woman announced proudly. "I bought that three-slice toaster you had on yesterday—there's just Bernie and Ray and me, now that Clyde's gone away to the Army—and my sister-in-law has four of the ceiling fans.''

In her head, Vanessa heard the production manager, Paul Harmon, giving his standard public relations lecture. *As the viewing audience expands, you'll be recognized. No matter what, I want you all to be polite at all times.*

''Good,'' she said with a faltering smile.

She took another look at her watch, then lost her cool and rammed the cash machine with the palms of her hands. Miraculously two twenty-dollar bills popped out of the appropriate slot, but Vanessa's cash card was disgorged in three pieces.

She dropped both the card and the money into the pocket of her linen blazer and dashed for the car, hoping the traffic wouldn't be bad.

It was.

Worse, when Vanessa reached her attorney's modest office, Parker was there with his lawyer and his current girlfriend.

Vanessa prayed she didn't look as frazzled as she felt and resisted an urge to smooth her chin-length auburn hair.

Parker smiled his dazzling smile and tried to kiss her cheek, but Vanessa stepped back, her golden eyes clearly telling him to keep his distance.

Her ex-husband, now the most sought-after pitcher in the American League, looked hurt. "Hello, Van," he said in a low and intimate voice.

Vanessa didn't speak. Although they had been divorced for a full year, Parker's presence still made her soul ache. It wasn't that she wanted him back; no, she grieved for the time and love she'd wasted on him.

Vanessa's attorney, Walter, was no ball of fire, but he was astute enough to know how vulnerable she felt. He drew back a chair for her near his desk, and gratefully she sank into the seat.

Parker's lawyer immediately took up the conversational ball. "I think we can settle this reasonably," he said. Vanessa felt her spine stiffen.

The bottom line was that Parker had been offered a phenomenal amount of money to write a book about his career in professional baseball and, with the help of a ghostwriter, he'd produced a manuscript—one that included every intimate detail of his marriage to Vanessa.

She was prepared to sue if the book went to press.

"Wait," Parker interceded suavely, holding his famous hands up in the air, "I think it would be better if Van and I worked this thing out ourselves . . . in private."

His girlfriend shifted uncomfortably on the leather sofa beside him, but said nothing.

"There is nothing to work out," Vanessa said in a shaky voice she hated. Why couldn't she sound detached and professional, like she did when she was selling ceiling fans on the Midas Network? "If you don't take me out of that book, Parker, I'm going to drive a dump truck into your bank account and come out with a load of your money."

Parker went pale beneath his golden tan. He ran a hand through his sun-streaked hair, and his azure blue eyes skittered away from Vanessa's gaze. But after a moment, he regained his legendary poise. "Van, you're being unreasonable."

"Am I? That book makes me sound like some kind of sex-crazed neurotic. I'm not going to let you ruin me, Parker, just so you can have a few more annuities and condominiums!"

Parker flinched as though she'd struck him. He rose from his chair and came to crouch before hers, speaking softly and holding both her hands in his. "You feel threatened," he crooned.

It was all Vanessa could do not to kick him. She jerked her hands free, shot to her feet and stormed out of the office.

Parker caught up to her at the elevator, which, as luck would have it, was just arriving. "Baby, wait," he pleaded.

Vanessa was shamed by the tears that were flowing down her face, but she couldn't stop them. She dodged into the elevator, trying to escape the man sportscasters compared to Hank Aaron and Pete Rose.

Parker squeezed into the cubicle with her, oblivious, apparently, of the fact that there were two secretaries, a cleaning woman and a bag lady looking on. He tried again, "Sweetheart, what do you want? A mink? A Corvette? Tell me what you want and I'll give it to you. But you've got to be reasonable!"

Vanessa drew her hand back and slapped the Living Legend. "How dare you assume you can buy me, you pompous jackass!" she cried. "And stop calling me sweetheart and baby!"

The elevator reached the ground floor, and Vanessa hurried out, hoping Parker wouldn't give chase. As it happened, however, he was right on her heels.

He looked exasperated now as he lengthened his strides to keep pace with her on the busy downtown sidewalk. He straightened the lapels of his tailored suit jacket and rasped out, "Damn it, Vanessa, do you know how much money is at stake here?"

"No, and I don't care," Vanessa answered. She was almost to the parking lot where she'd left her car; in a few minutes she could get behind the steering wheel and drive away.

With sudden harshness, Parker stopped her again, grasping her shoulders with his hands and pressing her backward against a department store display window. "You're not going to ruin this deal for me, Vanessa!" he shouted.

Vanessa stared at him, appalled and breathless. God knew Parker had hurt her often enough, but he'd never been physically rough.

Parker's effort to control his temper was visible. "I'm sorry," he ground out, and because he seldom apologized for anything, Vanessa believed him. "I didn't mean to manhandle you like that. Vanessa, please. Sit down with me somewhere private and listen to what I have to say. That's all I'm asking."

"There's no point, Parker," Vanessa replied. "I know what you want to tell me, and my answer

won't be any different. The way you portrayed me
in that book is libelous—I wouldn't be able to hold
my head up in public.''

''And I thought you'd be proud when I sent you
a copy of that manuscript.'' He paused to shake
his head, as if still amazed at her negative reaction. ''Van, people will know I made most of that
stuff up,'' Parker went on presently with a weak
smile. ''They're not going to take it seriously.''

Vanessa arched one eyebrow. ''Oh, really? Well,
I'd rather not take the chance, if you don't mind.
I have dreams of my own, you know.''

Passersby were beginning to make whispers that
indicated they recognized Parker. He took Vanessa's arm and squired her into a nearby coffee shop.
''Two minutes,'' he said. ''That's all I want.''

She smiled acidly. ''That's you, Parker—the
two-minute man.''

He favored her with a scorching look and
dropped into the booth's seat across from her.
''I'd forgotten what a little witch you can be,
Van.'' He paused to square his shoulders. ''Darla
hasn't complained.''

Darla, of course, was the girlfriend. ''People
with IQ's under twenty rarely do,'' Vanessa answered sweetly. Then she added, ''Your two minutes are ticking away.''

A waitress came, and Parker ordered two cups of coffee without even consulting Vanessa. It was so typical that she nearly laughed out loud.

"The advance on this book," Parker began in a low and reluctant voice, "is in the high six figures. I can't play baseball forever, Van; I need some security."

Vanessa rolled her eyes. Most oil sheiks didn't live as well as Parker; he certainly wasn't facing penury. "I'll drop you off at the food bank if you'd like," she offered.

A muscle bunched in his jaw. Vanessa could have lived for years on the money that Parker's face brought in for beer commercials alone. "You know," he said, "I really didn't expect you to be so bitter and frustrated."

The coffee arrived, and the waitress walked away again.

"Watch it," Vanessa warned. "You're trying to get on my good side, remember?"

Parker spread his hands in a gesture of baffled annoyance. "Van, I know the divorce was hard on you, but you have a job now and a life of your own. There's no reason to torture me like this."

He sounded so damnably rational that Vanessa wanted to throw her coffee in his face. "Is that what you think I'm doing? I want nothing from you, Parker—no money, no minks, no sports cars—and no lies written up in a book and presented as the truth.''

"So I was a little creative? What's wrong with that?"

"Nothing, if you're writing a novel." Vanessa could see that the conversation was progressing exactly as she'd expected. "I don't know why I even came down here," she said, glancing at her watch and sliding out of the booth.

"Hot date?" Parker asked, giving the words an unsavory inflection.

"Very hot," Vanessa lied, looking down at Parker. She was meeting her cousin Rodney for dinner and a movie, but what Parker didn't know wouldn't hurt him. She made a *sssssssss* sound, meant to indicate a sizzle, and walked away.

Much to her relief, Parker didn't follow.

Rodney was waiting in the agreed place when she reached the mall, his hands wedged into his jacket pockets, his white teeth showing in a grin.

"Hi, Van," he said. "Bad day?"

Vanessa kissed his cheek and linked her arm through his. "I just came from a meeting with Parker," she replied. "Does that answer your question?"

Rodney frowned. "Yeah," he said. "I'm afraid it does."

Vanessa smiled up at the handsome young man with the thick, longish chestnut brown hair and Omar Sharif eyes. Her first cousin—and at twenty-one, five years her junior—Rodney was the only family she had in Seattle, and she loved him. She changed the subject. "Aren't you going to ask me about the apartment?"

Rodney laughed as they walked into the mall together and approached their favorite fast-food restaurant, a place that sold Chinese cuisine to go. The apartment over Vanessa's garage was empty since her last tenant had moved out, and Rodney wanted the rooms in the worst way.

"You know I do, Van," he scolded her good-naturedly. "Living over a funeral home has its drawbacks. For one thing, it gives new meaning to the phrase, 'things that go bump in the night.'"

Van laughed and shook her head. "Okay, okay—you can move in in a few weeks. I want to have the place painted first."

Rodney's face lighted up. He was a good kid working his way through chiropractic school by means of a very demanding and unconventional job, and Vanessa genuinely enjoyed his company.

In fact, they'd always been close. "I'll do the painting," he said.

It was late when Vanessa arrived at the large colonial house on Queen Anne Hill and let herself in the front door. She crossed the sparsely furnished living room, kicking off her high heels and rifling through the day's mail as she moved.

In the kitchen, she flipped on the light and put a cup of water in the microwave to heat for tea. When the brew was steaming on the table, she steeled herself and pressed the button on her answering machine.

The first message was from her boss, Paul Harmon. "Janet and I want you to have dinner with us a week from Friday at DeAngelo's. Don't bring a date."

Vanessa frowned. The Harmons were friends of hers and they were forever trying to fix her up with one of their multitude of unattached male acquaintances. The fact that Paul had specified she shouldn't bring a date was unsettling.

She missed the next two messages, both of which were from Parker, because the name of the restaurant had rung a distant bell. What was it about DeAngelo's that made her uncomfortable?

She stirred sweetener into her tea, frowning. Then it came to her—the proprietor of the place was Nick DeAngelo, a former pro football player with a reputation for womanizing exceeded only by Parker's. Vanessa shuddered. The man was Paul's best friend. What if he turned out to be the mysterious fourth at dinner?

Vanessa shut off the answering machine and dialed the Harmons' home number. Janet answered the phone.

"About dinner at DeAngelo's," Vanessa said, after saying hi. "Am I being set up to meet Mr. Macho, or what?"

Janet laughed. "I take it you're referring to Nick?"

"And you're hedging," Vanessa accused.

"Okay, yes—we want you to meet Nick. He's a darling, Vanessa. You'll love him."

"That's what you said about that guy who wanted to take me parking," Vanessa reminded her friend. "I really don't think this is a good idea."

"He's nothing like Parker," Janet said gently. She could be very perceptive. "It isn't fair to write Nick off as a loser without even meeting him."

The encounter with Parker had inclined her toward saying no to everything, and Vanessa knew it. She sighed. She had to be flexible, willing to meet new people and try new things, or she'd become stagnant. "All right, but if he turns out to be weird, Janet Harmon, you and Paul are off my Christmas-card list for good."

That damned sixth sense of Janet's was still evident. "The appointment with Parker and his attorney went badly, huh?"

Vanessa took a steadying sip of her tea. "He's going to publish that damned book, Janet," she whispered, feeling real despair. "There isn't anything I can do to stop him, and I'm sure he knows it, even though he seems to feel some kind of crazy need to win me over to his way of thinking."

"The bastard," Janet commiserated.

"I can say goodbye to any hopes I had of ever landing a job as a newscaster. I'll never be taken seriously."

"It's late, and you're tired," Janet said firmly. "Take a warm bath, have a glass of wine and get some sleep. Things will look better in the morning."

Exhausted, Vanessa promised to take her friend's advice and went off to bed, stopping only to wash her face and brush her teeth. She collapsed onto the mattress and immediately fell into a troubled sleep, dreaming that Parker was chewing her cash card and spitting the plastic pieces out on the pitcher's mound.

She awakened the next morning in a terrible mood, and when she reached the studio complex where the Midas Network was housed, her co-host, Mel Potter, looked at her with concern in his eyes.

A middle-aged, ordinary looking man, Potter was known as Markdown Mel in the telemarketing business, and he was a pro's pro. He had ex-wives all over the country and a gift for selling that was unequaled in the field. Vanessa had seen him move two thousand telephone answering machines in fifteen minutes without even working up a sweat, and her respect for his skill as a salesman was considerable.

He was, in fact, the one man in the world, besides her grandfather, who could address her as honey without making her hackles rise.

"What's the matter, honey?" he demanded as Vanessa flopped into a chair in the makeup room. "You look like hell."

Vanessa smiled. "Thanks a lot, Mel," she answered. "You're a sight for sore eyes yourself."

He laughed as Margie, the makeup girl, slathered Vanessa's face with cleansing cream. "I see by the papers that that ex-husband of yours is in town to accept an award at his old high school. Think you could get him to stop by the studio before he leaves? We could dump a lot of those baseball cake plates if Parker Lawrence endorsed them.''

Now it was Vanessa who laughed, albeit a little hysterically. "Forget it, Mel. Parker and I aren't on friendly terms, and I wouldn't ask him for the proverbial time of day.''

Mel shrugged, but Vanessa had a feeling she hadn't heard the last of the subject of Parker Lawrence selling baseball cake plates.

Twenty minutes later Vanessa and Mel were on camera, demonstrating a set of golf clubs. Vanessa loved her job. Somehow, when she was working, she became another person—one who had no problems, no insecurities and no bruises on her soul.

The network had a policy of letting viewers chat with the hosts over the air, and the first caller was Parker.

"Hello, Babe," he said, after carefully introducing himself to the nation so that there could be no doubt as to who he was. "You look terrific.''

Vanessa's smile froze on her face. She tried to speak, but she couldn't.

Mel picked up the ball with admirable aplomb. "Thanks, Parker," he answered. "You look pretty good yourself.''

Even the cameraman laughed at that.

"Giving up baseball for golf?" Vanessa was emboldened to say.

"Never," Parker answered confidently. "But I'd take ten of anything you're selling, Baby."

Vanessa was seething inside, but she hadn't forgotten that several million people were watching and listening. She wasn't about to let Parker throw her in front of a national audience. "Good," she said, beaming. "We'll put you down for ten sets of golf clubs."

Parker laughed, thinking she was joking. Vanessa wished she could see his face when the UPS man delivered his purchases in seven to ten working days.

2

The man was impossibly handsome, Vanessa thought ruefully as she watched Nick DeAngelo approach the table where she and the Harmons had been seated. He was tall, with the kind of shoulders one might expect of a former star football player. His hair was dark and attractively rumpled as though he'd just run his fingers through it. But it was the expression in his eyes that took hold of something deep inside Vanessa and refused to let go.

Suddenly Vanessa's emotional scars, courtesy of Parker Lawrence, got the best of her. She could have sworn they were as visible as stitch marks across her face and she was positive that Nick DeAngelo could count them. Her first instinct was to run and hide.

Grinning, Paul stood to greet his friend. "You survived the flu," he remarked. "From the way you sounded, I didn't think you were going to make it."

A half smile curved Nick's lips, probably in acknowledgment of what Paul had said, but his gaze was fixed on Vanessa. He seemed to be unwrapping her soul, layer by layer, and she didn't want that. She needed the insulation to feel safe.

She dropped her eyes, color rising to her cheeks, and clasped her hands together in her lap. In a matter of moments, a decade of living, loving and hurting had dropped away. She was as vulnerable as a shy sixteen-year-old.

"Vanessa," Paul said gently, prodding her with his voice. "This is my friend, Nick DeAngelo."

She looked up again because she had to, and Nick was smiling at her. A strange sensation washed over her, made up of fear and delight, consolation and challenge. "Hello," she said, swallowing.

His smile was steady and as warm as winter fire. Vanessa was in over her head, and she knew it. "Hi," he replied, his voice low and deep.

The sound of it caressed the bruises on Vanessa's soul like a healing balm. She was frightened by his ability to touch her so intimately and wondered if anyone would believe her if she said she'd developed a headache and needed to go home to put her feet up. She started to speak, but Janet Harmon cut her off.

"I hear you're opening another restaurant in Portland next month," she said to Nick, her foot bumping against Vanessa's under the table. "Won't that take you out of town a lot?"

The phenomenal shoulders moved in an easy shrug. Nick DeAngelo was obviously as much at home in a tuxedo as he would be in a football jersey and blue jeans. His brown eyes roamed over Vanessa, revealing an amused approval of the emerald-green silk shirtwaist she was wearing. "I'm used to traveling," he said finally in response to Janet's question.

Vanessa devoutly wished that she'd stayed home. She wasn't ready for an emotional involvement, but it seemed to be happening anyway, without her say-so. She was as helpless as a swimmer going down for the third time. In desperation, she clasped on to the similarities between Parker and Nick.

They were both attractive, although Vanessa had to admit that Parker's looks had never affected her in quite the same way that Nick's were doing now. They were both jocks, and, if the press could be believed, Nick, like Parker, was a veritable legend among the bimbos of the world.

Vanessa felt better and, conversely, worse. She lifted her chin and said, "I don't think a jock—I mean, professional athlete ever gets the road completely out of his blood."

Nick sat back in his chair. His look said he could read her as clearly as a floodlighted billboard. "Maybe it's like selling electric foot massagers on television," he speculated smoothly. "I don't see how a person could ever put a thrill like that behind them."

Vanessa squirmed. How typically male; he knew she was responding to him, and now he meant to make fun of her. "I'm not ashamed of what I do for a living, Mr. DeAngelo," she said.

Nick bent toward her and, in that moment, it was as though the two of them were alone at the table—indeed, alone in the restaurant. "Neither am I, Ms. Lawrence," he replied.

A crackling silence followed, which was finally broken by Paul's diplomatic throat clearing and he said, "Vanessa hopes to anchor one of the local news shows at some point."

Vanessa winced, sure that Nick would be amused at such a lofty ambition. Instead he merely nodded.

Dinner that night was delicious, although Vanessa was never able to recall exactly what it was, for she spent every minute longing to run for cover. After the meal, the foursome drifted from the dining room to the crowded cocktail lounge, where a quartet was playing soft music. Vanessa found herself held alarmingly close to Nick as they danced.

He lifted her chin with a curved finger and spoke in a velvety rasp. "Your eyes are the size of satellite dishes. Do I scare you that much?"

Vanessa stiffened. The man certainly had an ego. "You don't scare me at all," she lied. "It's only that I'm—I'm tired."

He smiled, and the warmth threatened to melt her like a wax statue. "You were married to Parker Lawrence, weren't you?"

Suddenly it was too hot in the place; Vanessa felt as though she'd suffocate if she couldn't get some fresh air. "Yes," she answered, flustered, searching for an avenue of escape.

True to form, Nick read her thoughts precisely. "This way," he said, and, taking Vanessa by the hand, he led her off the dance floor, down a hallway and into a large, tastefully furnished office. She was about to protest when she realized there was a terrace beyond the French doors on the far side of the room.

The autumn night was chilly, but Vanessa didn't mind. The crisp air cleared her head, and she felt better immediately.

The sky was like a great black tent, pierced through in a million places by tiny specks of silver light, and the view of downtown Seattle and the harbor was spectacular. Vanessa rested her folded arms against the stone railing and drew a deep, delicious breath.

"It's beautiful," she said, smiling.

Nick was beside her, gazing at the city lights and moonlit water spread out below them. "I never get tired of it," he said quietly. "The only drawback is that you can't see the Space Needle from here."

Vanessa shivered as an icy breeze swept off the water, and Nick immediately draped his tuxedo jacket over her shoulders. She thanked him shyly with a look, and asked, "Have you lived in Seattle all your life?"

He nodded. "I was born here."

Vanessa marveled that she could be so comfortable with Nick on the terrace when she'd felt threatened inside the restaurant. She sighed. "I grew up in Spokane, but I guess I'm starting to feel at home."

"Just starting?" He arched a dark eyebrow.

Vanessa shrugged. "Seattle is Parker's home-town, not mine." Too late she realized she'd made a mistake, reopening a part of her life she preferred to keep private.

Nick leaned against the terrace and gazed at the circus of lights below. "I've been married before, too," he confided quietly. "Her name was Jenna."

Vanessa was practically holding her breath. It was incomprehensible that his answer should mean so much, but it did. "What happened?"

"She left me," Nick replied without looking at Vanessa.

"I'm sorry," Vanessa said, and she was sincere because she knew how much it hurt when a marriage died, whether a person was left or did the leaving. "A lot of women can't handle living with a professional athlete," she added, and although she'd meant the words as a consolation, she immediately wished she could take them back.

"Jenna bailed out before I got into the pros," Nick said in tones as cool as the wind rising off the water. "When I started making big bucks, she wanted to try again."

Before Vanessa could make any kind of response to that, Nick put an arm around her waist and ushered her back inside. She lifted the tuxedo jacket from her shoulders while he closed the French doors that led out onto the terrace.

"Did you love Jenna?" she asked, and the words were the most involuntary ones she'd ever spoken.

Nick's expression was unreadable. "Did you love Parker?" he countered.

Vanessa bit her lower lip. "I honestly don't know," she answered after a few moments of thought. "I was in college when I met him, and he was already breaking records in baseball. I'd never met anyone like him before. He was—overwhelming."

Nick grinned somewhat sadly and leaned back against the edge of his desk, his arms folded. "I'd like to know you better," he said.

Vanessa was aware that such straightforwardness was rare in a man, and she was impressed. She was also terrified by the powerful things this man was making her feel. She placed his jacket carefully over the back of a chair, searching her mind for a refusal that would not be rude or hurtful.

She was unprepared for Nick's sudden appearance at her side, and for the way he gently lifted her chin in his hand and said, "It's time to let go of the pain and move on, Vanessa."

The low, rumbling words, spoken so close to her mouth, made her lips tingle with a strange sense of anticipation. When Nick kissed her, she swayed slightly, stricken by a sweet malaise that robbed her of all balance.

Nick was holding her upright, though whether by means of the kiss or his gentle grasp on her waist, Vanessa couldn't be sure. She knew only that she was responding to him with her whole being, that she'd let him take her then and there if he pressed her. Being so vulnerable when she'd been so badly hurt before was almost more than she could bear.

When Nick finally released her, having kissed her more thoroughly than Parker ever had in even the most intimate of moments, she was so dazed that she could only stare up at him in abject amazement. She made up her mind that she absolutely would not see him again, no matter what.

He was too dangerous.

"Are you working tomorrow?" he asked in a sleepy voice, toying with a tendril of titian hair that had slipped from her ivory barrette.

Vanessa struggled to remember, her throat thick, her mind a razzle-dazzle of popping lights. Finally she shook her head.

Nick grinned. "Good. Will you spend the day with me.

No, no, no, cried Vanessa's wounded spirit. "Yes," she choked out.

Nick smiled at her, tracing the curve of her cheek with one index finger, then reached for his jacket and shrugged into it. "We'd better get back out there before Paul and Janet decide we're doing something in keeping with my image."

They went back to the dance floor, and Nick held her. It was an innocent intimacy but it stirred Vanessa's senses, which had been largely dormant for the better part of a year, to an alarming pitch of need.

Every time she dared to meet Nick's eyes, it was as though he had taken away an item of her clothing, and yet she could not resist looking at him. The dilemma was at once delicious and maddening, and Vanessa was relieved when Nick didn't offer to drive her home at the end of the evening.

Paul lingered on the sidewalk for a few minutes, talking with Nick, while Vanessa and Janet settled themselves in the car.

"Well," Janet demanded the moment she'd snapped her seat belt into place, "what did you think of him?"

Vanessa drew in a deep breath and let it out in an agitated rush. "I think I should have stayed home with my needlepoint," she said.

Janet turned in the car seat to look back at her. "You've got to be kidding. The man is a hunk!"

Only now, when her nostrils weren't filled with the subtle scent of his cologne and her body wasn't pressed to his could Vanessa be rational and objective where Nick DeAngelo was concerned. "He's also a jock," she said miserably. "Do you have any idea how egotistical those men can be? Not to mention callous and self-serving?"

Janet sighed. "Not every man is like Parker," she insisted.

The conversation was cut off at that point because Paul came back to the car, whistling cheerfully as he slid behind the wheel. Vanessa shrank into the corner of the seat, wishing, all in the same moment, that the night would end, that she could go back in time and say no to Nick's suggestion that they spend the next day together and that tomorrow would hurry up and arrive so she could see him again.

"Thanks," she said ruefully when Paul saw her to her door a few minutes later.

He smiled as she turned the key in the lock and pushed the door open. "Sounds as if you have mixed feelings about Nick," he commented.

Vanessa kicked off her high heels the moment she'd crossed the threshold. "I have *no* feelings about Nick," she argued, facing Paul but keeping her eyes averted. "Absolutely none."

Her boss chuckled. "Good night, Van," he said, and then he was gone, striding back down the front walk to his car.

Vanessa locked the door, slipped out of her velvet evening coat and bent to pick up her discarded shoes. Her calico cat, Sari, curled around her ankles, meowing.

Sari had already had her supper, and even though she had a weight problem, Vanessa couldn't turn a deaf ear to her plaintive cries. She set her purse, coat and shoes down on the deacon's bench in the hallway and allowed herself to be herded into the kitchen.

Even before she flipped on the lights, she saw the blinking red indicator on the answering machine. Vanessa was in no mood to deal with relationships of any kind that night; she wanted to feed the cat and go to bed. Her own innate sense of responsibility—some calamity could have be fallen Rodney or her aging grandparents—made her cross the room and push the play button.

She was opening a can of cat food and scraping it into Sari's dish when Parker's voice filled the kitchen.

The first message was relatively polite, but, as the tape progressed, Parker grew more and more irate. Finally he flared, "Don't you ever stay home? Damn it, call me!"

Vanessa had washed her hands and was about to turn off the machine when Nick's voice rolled over her like a warm, rumbling wave. "You're a terrific lady," he said. "I'm looking forward to seeing you again tomorrow."

Vanessa moaned faintly and sank into a chair, propping her chin in both hands. With a few idle words, the man had melted the muscles in her knees.

"Good night," he said, his voice deep and gentle, and then the tape was silent.

After a few moments of sheer bewilderment, Vanessa got up and checked the locks on both the front and back doors. Then, taking her coat and shoes with her, Sari padding along beside her, she went upstairs.

She hung her coat carefully in the closet and put the shoes back into their plastic box. Soon she was in bed, but sleep eluded her.

She kept imagining what it would be like to lie beside Nick DeAngelo, in this bed or any other, and have him touch her, kiss her, make love to her. Just the thought made her ache.

Sometime toward morning, Vanessa slept. The telephone awakened her to a full complement of sunshine, and she grappled for the receiver, losing it several times before she managed to maneuver it into place.

"Hello," she accused, shoving one hand through her rumpled hair and scowling.

After knowing him such a short time, it seemed impossible, but she recognized Nick's laughter. "Don't tell me, let me guess. You're not a morning person."

Vanessa narrowed her eyes to peer at the clock and saw that it was nearly nine o'clock. She was glad Nick had called, she decided, because that gave her a chance to cancel their date. "Listen, I've been thinking—"

He cut her off immediately. "Well, stop. You've obviously in no condition for that kind of exertion. I'll be over in ten minutes to ply you with coffee."

"Nick!" Vanessa cried, afraid of being plied. But it was too late, he'd already hung up and she had no idea what his home telephone number was.

Grumbling, she got out of bed, stumbled into the bathroom and took a shower. By the time Nick arrived, she was clad in jeans and a blue bulky knit sweater and was fully conscious.

She greeted him at the front door, holding a cup of therapeutically strong coffee in one hand. "You didn't give me a chance to tell you on the phone, but..."

Nick grinned in that disarming way he had and assessed her trim figure with blatant appreciation. "Good, you're dressed," he said, walking past her into the house.

"You expected me to be naked?" Vanessa wanted to know.

He laughed. "I'm allowed my share of fantasies, aren't I?"

Vanessa shook her head. Nick was impossible to shun. He was wearing jeans and a hooded sweatshirt, and he had the look of a man who knew where he was going to spend that chilly, sun-washed Saturday. "Come in, come in," she chimed wryly as he preceded her down the hallway to the kitchen. "Don't be shy."

He grinned at her over one shoulder. "I've never been accused of that," he assured her.

Vanessa had no doubt he was telling the truth. She gave up. "Where are we going?"

"Running," he said. "Then I thought we'd take in a movie. . . ."

Vanessa was holding up both hands in a demand for silence. "Wait a minute, handsome—rewind to the part about running."

Nick dragged his languorous brown eyes from the toes of her sneakers to the crown of her head. "Bad idea? You certainly look like someone who cares about fitness."

She sighed and poured her coffee into the sink. "Thank you—I think."

"I guess we could skip running—just for today," he said, stepping closer to her.

Vanessa's senses went on red alert, and she leaped backward as though he'd burned her. "On second thought, running sounds like a great idea," she said, in a squeaky voice, embarrassed. "You seem to have a lot of—of extra energy."

He favored her with slow, sensuous grin. "Oh, believe me," he said with quiet assurance, "I do."

Vanessa swallowed. It was beyond her how accepting a single blind date could get a person into so much trouble. She swore to herself that the next time Janet and Paul wanted to introduce her to someone, she was going to hide in the cellar until the danger passed.

"Relax," Nick said, approaching and taking her shoulders into his big, gentle hands. "You are one tense individual, Value Van."

Vanessa blinked. "What did you call me?"

"I've gotten kind of caught up in this cable marketing thing," he replied, his dark eyes twinkling. "I thought you should have a professional nickname, like your friend Markdown Mel. The possibilities are endless, you know—there's Bargain Barbara, for instance, and Half-price Hannah..."

Vanessa began to laugh. "I never know whether to take you seriously or not."

He bent his head and kissed her, innocently and briefly. "Oh, you should take me seriously, Van. It's the rest of your life that needs mellowing out."

She gave him a shove. "Let's go running," she said.

They drove to the nearest park in Nick's Corvette. He led the way to the jogging path and immediately started doing stretching exercises.

Vanessa eyed him ruefully, then began, in her own awkward fashion, to follow suit. "One thing about dating a jock," she ventured to say, breathing a little hard as she tried to keep up with his bends and stretches, "a girl stays skinny, no matter what."

Nick started off down the path after rolling his eyes once, and Vanessa was forced to follow at a wary trot. "Are you saying that I'm not a fun guy?" he asked over one shoulder.

"What could be more fun than this?" Vanessa countered, already gasping for breath. She'd dropped her exercise program during the divorce, and the effects of her negligence were painfully obvious.

When they reached a straight stretch, Nick turned and ran backward, no trace of exertion visible in his manner or voice. "So, how long have you been a member of the loyal order of couch potatoes?" he asked companionably.

"I hate you," huffed Vanessa.

"That really hurts, Value Van," Nick replied. "See if I ever buy another pair of Elvis Presley bookends from you."

There was grass alongside the pathway, and Vanessa flung herself onto it, dragging air into her lungs and groaning. She couldn't believe she was there in the park, torturing herself this way when she could have slept in until noon and sent out for Chinese food.

Nick did not keep running, as she'd expected. Instead he flopped down on the cold grass beside her and said, "I appreciate the offer, but we haven't known each other long enough."

Vanessa gave him a look and clambered to her feet. "Tired so soon?" she choked out, jogging off down the pathway.

At the end of the route, which Vanessa privately thought of as The Gauntlet, the ice-blue Corvette sat shining in the autumn sunlight. She staggered toward it and collapsed into the passenger seat while Nick was still cooling down.

When he slid behind the wheel, she barely looked at him. "What did I do to Janet to make her hate me like this?" she asked.

Nick chuckled and started the car. "I'll answer that when I've had a shower."

Vanessa's eyes flew open wide. Showering was an element she hadn't thought about, even though it seemed perfectly obvious now.

Nick's expression was suddenly serious. "Relax, Van," he said. "It's a private shower, and you're not invited."

To her everlasting chagrin, Vanessa blushed like a Victorian schoolgirl. She was a reserved person, but not shy. She wondered again what it was about this man that circumvented all the normal rules of her personality and made her act like someone she didn't even know.

"It never crossed my mind that you might expect me to share a shower with you," Vanessa lied, her chin at a prim angle, her arms folded.

"Liar," Nick replied with amused affection.

He lived in a condominium on the top floor of one of the most historic buildings in Seattle, and the place had a quiet charm that surprised Vanessa. She had expected a playboy's den with lots of velvet, chrome and smoked glass, but the spacious rooms were decorated in earth tones instead. There was an old-fashioned fireplace in the living room and a beautiful Navaho rug graced the wall above the cushy beige corduroy sofa.

"Make yourself at home," Nick said casually, ducking through a doorway and leaving Vanessa to stand there alone, feeling sweaty and rumpled and totally out of place.

She went to the window and looked out on busy Elliot Bay. A passenger ferry was chugging into port, large and riverboatlike, and Vanessa smiled. In the distance, she heard the sound of running water and an off-key rendition of a current popular song.

The view kept her occupied for what seemed like a long time, but when Nick didn't return after ten minutes, Vanessa began to grow uneasy. She approached the big-screen television in one corner of the room and pushed the On button.

Immediately the Midas Network leaped out at her in living color, life-size. She turned the set off again and began to pace, tempted to sneak out before this nonrelationship with Nick DeAngelo grew into something she couldn't handle.

She was just reaching for the doorknob when his voice stopped her.

"Don't go," he said quietly. "I'm not going to hurt you in any way, Vanessa. I swear it."

She couldn't move, couldn't drop her hand to her side or turn the knob and make her escape.

"Something really important is happening here," he went on. "Can't you feel it?"

Vanessa let her forehead rest against the cool panel of the door. "Yes," she confessed in a strangled voice, "and that's what scares me."

He stepped closer to her and laid his hands very gently on her shoulders. She was filled with the scent of his clean hair, his freshly washed skin. "I won't let anything happen that you're not ready for," he promised, and when he turned her around to face him, Vanessa was powerless to resist.

She looked up at him with eyes full of trust and fear, and he let his hands drop to her waist. He was careful not to hold her too close, and yet she was achingly aware of his total, unreserved masculinity.

"I'm going to kiss you," he said matter-of-factly. "That is, if you're ready."

She slid her arms around his neck and stood on tiptoe, exhilarated and, at the same time, terrified. "I'm ready," she answered, her mouth only a whisper away from his.

3

"Want a shower now?"

Vanessa, her energy drained by the kiss, had sagged back against the door when it was over. Her eyes opened wide, however, when Nick's words registered. "I beg your pardon?"

He turned and walked off toward the open kitchen, looking too good for comfort in his jeans and cut-off shirt. His stomach muscles made hard ripples when he lifted his arm to open a cupboard door, and Vanessa felt vaguely dizzy.

At that moment there was only one thing in the world she wanted more than a shower. She followed him, careful to keep the breakfast bar between them. "I don't have any clean clothes to put on," she ventured to say.

Nick shrugged. "Some of Gina's things are still here. You're about her size, I think."

The name made Vanessa round the breakfast bar. "Gina?" she asked, looking up at him.

He kissed her forehead. "My sister," he assured her.

The relief Vanessa felt was embarrassing in its scope. "I've never had to shower on a date before," she confessed.

Nick chuckled at that. "Never?"

Vanessa looked up into his dancing eyes and felt a painful tug somewhere in the region of her heart. She wanted to appear glamorous and sophisticated, but the truth was far different. She'd never been with any man besides Parker, and, when and if she went to bed with Nick, it was going to be almost like reliving the first time. At last she shook her head and answered, "Never."

He started to put his arms around her and then stopped. "Do you like Chinese food?" he asked.

Vanessa nodded.

"Good. You'll find the clothes and the shower down the hall—first room on the right. I'll go get our lunch while you're changing—okay?"

"Okay," Vanessa answered, not knowing quite what to make of this man. She knew Nick was attracted to her, and yet when he had an advantage, he didn't press it.

The room Nick had directed her to was large, though it obviously wasn't the place where he slept. There was a private bathroom, however, and

Vanessa locked herself in before stripping off the clothes she'd worn to run in the park.

When she finished showering, she found the promised clothes in closets and bureaus and finally helped herself to a jumpsuit of navy corduroy. She buttoned it to her eyeballs and was just entering the living room when Nick returned with cartons of fragrant sweet-and-sour chicken, chow mein and fried rice.

He smiled and shook his head when he saw the jumpsuit. "Feel better?" he asked.

Vanessa felt a number of things, and she wasn't ready to talk about any of them. She went to the cupboards and opened doors until she found plates for their food. They ate at the breakfast bar, perched on stools, and Nick insisted on using chopsticks.

"Show off," Vanessa said, spearing a succulent morsel of chicken with her fork.

He surprised her by laying down his chopsticks, reaching out and unfastening the top two buttons of the jumpsuit. "The weather's getting nasty outside," he commented, "but it's warm enough in here."

Vanessa blushed, embarrassed. She knew Nick thought she was a hidebound prude, but she didn't have the nerve to prove she wasn't. Not yet.

He leaned over and gave her a nibbling kiss on the lips. "Everything is okay, Van," he promised her quietly. "Just relax."

A light rain spattered the windows, and Nick left his stool to light a fire on the hearth. The crackling sound was cozy, and the colorful blaze gave that corner of the room a cheery glow.

Something Vanessa could not name or define made her leave her place at the breakfast bar and approach Nick. She knelt beside him, facing the fireplace, and said, "I'm not like you p-probably think I am. It's just that you scare me so much."

He turned to her, smiling softly, and slid four fingers into her hair, caressing her cheek with his thumb. "I won't tell you any lies, Vanessa," he replied. "I want you—I have since I turned on the Midas Network and saw you standing there with a toll-free number printed across your chest—but I'm willing to wait."

"Wait?" Vanessa asked. Nothing in her relationship with Parker had ever prepared her for this kind of patience from a man. He had to want something. "You're admitting, then, that there is a plan of seduction?"

He laughed. "Absolutely. I intend to make you want me, Vanessa Lawrence."

Vanessa figured he had the battle half won already, but she wasn't about to say that to him. In fact, she didn't say anything, because Nick De-Angelo had rendered her speechless.

He got up, leaving her kneeling there by the fire, and returned after a few minutes with two glasses of wine. After handing one to Vanessa and setting his own down on the brick hearth, he glanced pensively toward the rain-sheeted windows. "Do you want to go out to a movie, or shall we stay here?"

Even though Vanessa was still wishing that she'd stayed home, indeed that she'd never met Nick at all, she had no desire to leave the comfort and warmth of his fire. She was, in fact, having some pretty primitive and elemental feelings where he and his comfortable home were concerned. It was almost as though she'd been wandering, cold and hungry and alone, and he'd rescued her and brought her to a secret, special place that no one else knew about.

Vanessa shook her head. She hadn't even had a sip of her wine yet, and it was already getting to her.

"Van?" Nick prompted, peering into her face, and she realized that she hadn't answered his question.

"Oh. Yes. I mean, I'd like to sit by the fire and watch the storm." Even as she spoke, blue-gold lightning streaked across the angry sky and a fresh spate of rain pelted the glass.

Nick came back and sat down beside her on the rug. "Tell me about your life, Van," he said, his voice low.

She immediately tensed, but before she could frame a reply, Nick reached out and squeezed her hand.

"I'm not asking about Parker—I know a little about him because we traveled in some of the same circles. You're the one I'm curious about."

Vanessa took a sip of her wine and then told Nick the central facts about her childhood; that her father had died when she was seven, that her very young mother had been overwhelmed by responsibilities and grief and had left her daughter with her parents so that she could marry a rodeo cowboy. There had been cards, letters and the occasional Christmas and birthday gifts, but Van had rarely seen her mother after that.

The expression in Nick's eyes was a soft one as he listened, but there was no pity in evidence, and Vanessa appreciated that. Her childhood had been difficult, but there were lots of people who would have gladly traded places with her, and she had made a good life for herself—generally speaking.

"You've always wanted to be on television?" Nick asked, plundering the white paper bag he'd brought home from the Chinese restaurant until he found two fortune cookies at the bottom.

Vanessa sighed and shook her head. "Not really. I wanted to be Annie Oakley until I was six—then I made the shattering discovery that there was very little call for trick riding and fancy shooting except in the circus."

Nick grinned at that. "My childhood dream pales by comparison. I wanted to run my Uncle Guido's fish market."

Vanessa laughed. "And you had to settle for a career in professional football. My God, DeAngelo, that's sad—I don't know how you bore up under the disappointment!"

He had drawn very close. "I'm remarkable," he answered with a shrug.

"I can imagine," Vanessa confessed, and as he touched the sensitive, quivering flesh of her neck with his warm and tentative lips, she gave a little moan. "Is this the part where you start making me want you?" she dared to ask.

Nick nipped at her earlobe and chuckled when she trembled. "Yes. But that's all, so don't get nervous."

"What about what you want?" Vanessa asked.

"I can wait," he replied, and she knew she should push him away, but she couldn't. The attention he was giving her neck felt entirely too good.

Presently his hands came back to the buttons of the jumpsuit. Vanessa closed her fingers over his, realizing with a sleepy sort of despair that she wasn't wearing either bra or panties beneath the worn blue corduroy, but Nick would not be stopped. He was a gentle conqueror, though, and she had no more thoughts of fear or of escape.

She was lying on her back before the popping fire when he bared her breasts and watched the shimmer of the blaze and the flash of lightning play over them. Vanessa had never felt so feminine, so desirable.

With a low, grumbling groan, Nick lowered himself to chart the circumference of her breast with a whisperlight passing of his lips. Vanessa watched in delicious dread as he moved toward the peak he meant to conquer, in an upward spiraling pattern of kisses. A whimper of long-denied pleasure escaped her as he touched her budding nipple with his tongue, causing it to blossom like some lovely, exotic flower.

Beyond the windows, lightning raged against the sky as though seeking to thrust its golden fingers through the glass and snatch the lovers up in fire and heat. Vanessa shuddered involuntarily as Nick's hand made a slow, comforting circle on her belly, his lips and tongue continuing to master her nipple.

He'd said his goal was to make her want him, and he'd succeeded without question. Vanessa longed to give him the kind of intolerable pleasure he was giving her, to be joined with him in a fevered battle that would have no losers. But he was setting the pace, and Vanessa had no power to turn the tables.

Her breasts were moist and pleasantly swollen by the time he brought his mouth back to hers and consumed her in a kiss as elemental as the lightning tearing at the afternoon sky.

"Do you want me to make love to you, Van?" Nick whispered against her throat when the kiss had at last ended.

Vanessa could barely lie still, her body was so hungry for his. "Yes," she admitted breathlessly, her fingers frantic in his hair. "Oh, yes."

He gave a heavy sigh and circled a pulsing nipple with the tip of his tongue before saying the unbelievable words. "You're not ready for that, darlin'."

Although he'd spoken without a trace of malice, Vanessa still felt as though she'd been slapped. "You can't just—just leave me like this. . . ."

"Don't worry," he said, still toying with her nipple. "I don't intend to."

Moments later, he drew the jumpsuit down over her hips and legs and tossed it away. He kissed Vanessa thoroughly before trailing his mouth down over her collarbone, her breasts, her belly.

When he reached his destination, the lightning would wait no longer. It reached into the room, scooping Vanessa up with crackling fingers and bouncing her mercilessly in its palm. Only when she cried out in primitive satisfaction did it set her back on the rug in front of Nick's fireplace and leave her in relative peace.

She was crying, and she couldn't bring herself to look at the man who had unchained the lightning.

He covered her gently with an afghan as though she were a casualty of some sort and kissed her on the forehead. "I'll be back in a few minutes," he said.

By the time Nick returned, Vanessa had rallied enough to get back into the jumpsuit. She was standing at the window, looking out on the gloomy spectacle of a city dressed in twilight gray, hugging herself. Nick stood behind her, putting his arms around her, and she felt the chilly dampness of his bare chest against her back and guessed that he'd taken a cold shower.

"Why?" she asked, not looking at him because she couldn't. "I would have given myself to you. Didn't you want me?"

"Oh, I wanted you all right."

"Then why? Why didn't you take me?"

"Because this is your time, Vanessa. Because I think you're hiding somewhere deep inside yourself and you need to be coaxed into the world again. That's what I want to show you—that it's safe out here."

She turned in his arms, sliding hers around his waist. He wore nothing but a pair of jeans and an impudent half grin. She rested her forehead against his cool, muscular chest.

"It was as though the storm came inside," she confessed. "I've never felt anything like it."

Nick simply held her and listened.

"I'm not some kind of neurotic, you know," she went on. "And I'm not a prude, either."

He chuckled, and his lips moved softly at her temple. "No prude would have responded the way you did."

Vanessa looked up at him. "You were right earlier, Nick DeAngelo—you are a remarkable man."

He favored her with a cocky grin. "You have no idea how remarkable," he teased.

"I think I'd like to go home before I decide to find out," Vanessa replied.

Nick didn't argue, get insulted or try to convince her to stay. He simply put on a shirt and shoes, got her a paper bag for her jeans and sweater and drove her home.

"Will you come to dinner on Friday night?" Vanessa asked him, when they were standing in her kitchen and he'd just given her a goodbye kiss that brought faint flickers of lightning to her mind.

"Do I have to wait that long to see you again?" he countered, albeit good-naturedly.

Vanessa nodded. "I'm afraid so. If you're around, I won't get any rest at all, and when that happens, I don't do well on television."

Nick touched the tip of her nose with an index finger. "Okay." He sighed. "I'll content myself with watching you sell cordless screwdrivers and videotape rewinders for a week, but be forewarned, when Friday night comes around, you're in for another lesson on why I'm the only man for you."

Vanessa felt a pleasant little thrill at the prospect and hoped he didn't notice. "Eight o'clock," she said.

He kissed her again. "Seven, and I'll bring the wine."

"Seven-thirty," Vanessa negotiated, "and you can also build the fire."

Nick laughed. "Deal," he said, shaking her hand. And then he was gone, and Vanessa's big, empty house seemed bigger and emptier than ever.

She fed Sari, who had been telling a long and woeful tale in colloquial meows from the moment Vanessa and Nick had entered the house. She had just tossed her jeans, sweater and underwear into the utility room when someone began pounding at the front door.

Thinking Nick had come back, she hurried through the house, worked the lock and pulled the door open wide.

Parker was standing on the step, looking apoplectic. "Do you realize how many messages I've left for you since last night?" he demanded furiously.

Not wanting the neighbors to witness a domestic drama of the sort they'd learned to expect and relish during the last days of the marriage, Vanessa grasped Parker by the arm and pulled him inside the house.

"I've been busy," she hissed, annoyed. She started off toward the kitchen again, leaving Parker to follow. "What did you want, anyway?" she demanded, reaching into a cupboard for two mugs and marching over to the sink.

"I'm going to be on a talk show day after tomorrow," her ex-husband answered in grudging tones, hurling himself into a chair at the table. He named a very famous host. "She wants you to appear, too, since you're in the book."

So that was it. Vanessa's feelings of being cherished was displaced by a sensation of weariness. She wondered who, besides Parker, would have had the gall to suggest such a thing.

"No way, slugger," she breathed, setting the mugs full of water in the microwave and getting out a jar of instant coffee.

"It will mean more sales, Van," Parker whined, "and more sales means more money!"

Vanessa was standing by the counter, her arms folded, waiting for the water to heat. "You live in a fantasy world, don't you, Parker? A place where nobody ever says no to anything you want. Well, listen to this—I'm not going to help you promote that book, I'm going to sue you for writing it!''

The bell on the microwave chimed, and Vanessa took the mugs out and made coffee by rote. She set one in front of Parker with a thump and sat down on the opposite side of the table from him.

He was staring at the corduroy jumpsuit in baffled distaste. ''Good grief, Vanessa,'' he said, ''don't you make enough money to dress decently? Whatever that thing is, it's a size too big.''

Vanessa sighed. Some things never changed. ''I knew you were coming over and I dressed for the occasion,'' she said sweetly, taking a sip from her mug. Sari made a furry pass around her ankles, as if to lend reassurance.

Parker was a master of the quicksilver technique, and he sat back in his chair and smiled warmly at Vanessa. ''I hope I didn't make you feel inadequate,'' he said.

He'd made a specialty of it in the past, but Vanessa had no desire to hash over the bad old days. She thought of the hours she'd spent in Nick DeAngelo's company and smiled back. ''That's about the last thing I'm feeling right now,'' she answered.

Parker looked disappointed. "Oh."

Vanessa laughed at his frank bewilderment. "Listen," she said after recovering herself, "our marriage has been over for a long time. We don't have to do battle anymore."

He sat up straight. "The things I'm asking for are very simple, Vanessa," he said, sounding almost prim.

"And they're also impossible. I'm not going on any talk show to promote a book I'd like to see fade into obscurity."

His expression turned smug. "Suing me will only make sales soar," he said.

"I know," Vanessa confessed with a sigh. "Just tell me one thing, Parker—why did you describe me that way? Was that the kind of wife you wish I'd been?"

Parker averted his eyes, then pulled back the sleeve of his expensive Irish woolen sweater to glance at his Rolex. "What would I have to do to get you back?" he asked without even looking at her.

Vanessa was thunderstruck. Not once in her wildest imaginings had it ever occurred to her that Parker had been harassing her in a sort of schoolboy attempt to get her attention. She put her hands to her cheeks, unable for the moment to speak.

At last Parker met her gaze. "I thought things would be so much better without you," he told her gruffly. "Instead my whole life is going to hell."

Vanessa resisted an urge to take out the brandy she'd used to make fruitcake the year before and pour a generous dose into her coffee. "I'm flattered," she said in a moderate voice, "but I don't think getting back together would be good for either of us."

"You're in love with somebody else," Parker accused.

It was too soon to say that what Vanessa felt for Nick was love, but his appearance in her life had made some profound changes. "That's got nothing to do with anything," she answered. "There is no future for you and me—there shouldn't even have been a past." She got out of her chair and went to the back door, opening it to the chilly autumn wind and standing there looking at Parker.

To his credit, he took the hint and slid back his chair. "If you'd just let me stay, I could prove to you that getting divorced was a mistake for us."

Vanessa shook her head, marveling. "Good night," she said, and she closed and locked the door the moment Parker stepped over the threshold.

The telephone rang just as she was taking their cups from the table to the sink.

"Was that The Living Legend I just saw leaving your place?" her cousin Rodney demanded.

Vanessa smiled, looking out the kitchen window at the lighted apartment over the garage. "Yes. All moved in, are you?"

"Absolutely," Rodney replied. "I've been painting all day, and the fact is, I think if I close my eyes tonight I'm going to wake up asphyxiated."

"If you're asphyxiated, you don't usually wake up," Vanessa pointed out.

"I'd forgotten how nitpicky you get when you're tired," Rodney teased. "Are you going to invite me to sleep on your couch tonight or what?"

Vanessa laughed. "I haven't got a couch, remember? Parker took it. But you're welcome to spread out a sleeping bag and breathe free."

"I'll be right down," came the immediate response.

Rodney arrived within seconds, carrying a rolled-up sleeping bag and a paper sack with the name of a favorite delicatessen emblazoned on the side. "Have you had dinner?" he asked.

Vanessa realized that she hadn't had anything to eat since the Chinese lunch at Nick's, and she was hungry. "Actually, no," she answered.

Rodney pulled out the cutting board and slid the biggest hero sandwich Vanessa had seen in recent memory out of the bag. Her cousin reached for a knife and cut the huge combination of bread and lettuce, cheese and turkey into two equal pieces. "Share and share alike," he said.

Grinning, Vanessa took plates from the cupboard and brought them over to the counter. "I'm overwhelmed by your generosity."

"It's the least I can do for the woman who saved me from spending another night above Jergenson's Funeral Parlor," he replied.

Vanessa put half the sandwich onto her plate and went back to the table. "Someday, when you're a successful chiropractor, you'll look back on living there as a growth experience."

Rodney dropped into the chair directly across from hers. "You're trying to evade the real issue here, which is what did Parker want?"

"I don't think he knows," Vanessa confided, dropping her eyes to her sandwich.

"Damn," Rodney marveled, "he's trying to get you back, isn't he? I wonder how he found out you were seeing Nick DeAngelo. Bet it's eating him up—"

Vanessa gazed directly at her cousin. "How do you know about Nick?" she broke in.

"I saw him," Rodney answered with a shrug. "I go out with his sister Gina sometimes."

Vanessa blushed, remembering that she was wearing Gina's jumpsuit and wondering if Rodney recognized it. "Then you know him?" she speculated.

Rodney shrugged again. "You could say that, I guess. I've been on a few family picnics—when that tribe heads for the island, it's like some kind of Italian exodus."

Vanessa swallowed a weary giggle. "The island?" she asked, trying to sound casual.

The mischievous look in Rodney's eyes said she'd failed roundly. "Nick owns a big Victorian house in the San Juans," he answered. "Don't you ever read the tabloids? He's famous for the parties he gives."

A picture came into Vanessa's mind, the image of herself walking into Parker's condominium on Maui, planning to surprise him by arriving for their vacation a day ahead of time. She'd surprised him, all right—along with the Polynesian beauty sharing his bed.

Her thoughts turned to the storm of that afternoon, and the searing, crackling lightning. Vanessa felt betrayed.

The fiery gentleness of Nick's lovemaking had eased many of her doubts about him, but now she realized that the patience and caring he'd shown had probably been nothing more than pretense. If he liked to party and play the field, a relationship with her wasn't likely to change him any more than it had changed Parker.

Every self-help book on the market was screaming the message that men are an as-is proposition, once a rogue, always a rogue.

Vanessa put her hands over her face, her appetite gone.

"Van?" Rodney sounded worried. "What's the matter? Are you okay?"

Vanessa got out of her chair, carried her sandwich to the counter, wrapped it carefully and tucked it into the refrigerator. Although she didn't say a word, she was shaking her head the whole time.

Rodney's chair scraped against the floor as he pushed it back. "I said something wrong, didn't I?"

"No," Vanessa said, unable to meet her cousin's eyes, "you brought me to my senses, that's all. I'd forgotten that a jock is a jock is a jock." She paused at the base of the back stairway, her hand resting on the banister. "Good night," she said.

Words, Vanessa discovered, did not make it so. The night was not a good one, and the morning showed every sign of being worse.

4

The porcelain statuette of a Grecian goddess toppled precariously when Vanessa bumped into it, and it would have shattered on the studio floor if Mel hadn't been so quick to grab it.

Paul Harmon signaled from off-camera, and Vanessa was grateful for the respite.

"Are you all right?" her friend and employer asked, when she left Mel to sell the goddess unaided.

Vanessa drew a deep breath and let it out slowly. She'd been a klutz all morning, crashing into props and sales items, saying nonsensical things, getting prices and details wrong. She splayed her fingers and shoved them through her hair, thus spoiling the coiffure Margie in Makeup had spent twenty minutes styling. "Let's just say I'll be glad when this day is over." She sighed loudly.

Paul grinned. "Nick?" he asked.

Vanessa squared her shoulders. *What egotists men are,* she thought. *One of them comes along and screws up your life, and all his friends think what a guy.* "Nick who?" she countered coolly, turning around and marching back on camera.

An elderly lady from Tucson, calling in to order the statuette for her daughter, was on the air. "I've got all my credit cards up to their limits, but I can't help myself," she enthused. "I just had to get Venus for Allison. She'll love this for her bathroom."

Distracted, Vanessa forgot the cardinal telemarketing rule and said worriedly, "Maybe you shouldn't buy anything for a while. After all, there will be other statues, and you've worked hard to build up your credit. . . ."

Mel looked at Van as though her nose had just grown an inch and elbowed her aside. "Vanessa's kidding, of course," he boomed in his best it's-me-and-you-against-those-guys-who-charge-high-prices voice. "This is a unique piece of art that would grace anybody's bathroom."

Paul was signaling again, but this time he didn't look quite so friendly. When Vanessa reached him, he took her arm and squired her into the makeup room, where fast-talking Oliver Richards was being prepared to go on.

He glanced up at the monitor to let Vanessa know he'd witnessed her gaffe and wriggled his eyebrows. Since the day he'd made a pass at her and she'd set him straight, Oliver had taken pleasure in every setback she suffered, be it major or minor.

"Good work, Van," he said. "Keep this up, and we'll all be in the unemployment line."

Paul gave the former sportscaster a dark look. "Go out and take over for Mel. He's got a dental appointment and has to leave early." Oliver immediately left.

Vanessa lowered her head, braced for a lecture. "My mind hasn't been on my work this morning," she said. "I'm sorry."

Paul sighed. "This kind of thing happens to everybody at one point or another," he reasoned. "One thing is a given—the board isn't going to be pleased about that little speech you just made. Van, what possessed you to do that?"

"I told you, I wasn't thinking." Vanessa looked up at her friend, feeling defensive. "Besides, what I said was true, even if it wasn't a good sales technique. There are a lot of people out there running themselves into serious debt so they can put statues of Venus in their bathrooms."

"And I should pity the wretched masses and shut down the cameras?" Paul shot back, annoyed. "Is everybody supposed to do without the convenience of home shopping because a few people can't control themselves?"

"I didn't say that!" Vanessa cried.

Just then Nick walked in, looking reprehensibly handsome in gray slacks, a navy blue sweater and a charcoal sports jacket.

"What are you doing here?" Vanessa demanded.

"I'm going out to lunch with a friend," he answered calmly, his eyes dancing with amusement.

"We agreed not to see each other again until Friday," she reminded him.

"You're not the friend," Nick replied in reasonable tones. He looked over her head at Paul. "Ready to go, old buddy?"

Vanessa's face was flushed, and she turned away to hide it. "I'm due on camera," she muttered, striding purposefully toward the door.

"Try not to put us out of business before your segment's over," Paul called after her.

Although Vanessa was seething inside, she smiled at America and at Oliver Richards when she stepped back onto the set. A rowing machine had been brought on as the next item to be featured, and Oliver beamed as an idea came to mind.

"The lovely Vanessa Lawrence rejoins us, folks," he announced. "Just in time to demonstrate the rowing machine."

Determined not to lose her composure, Van kicked off her high heels and sat down on the machine's seat, trying to be graceful as she tugged the straight skirt of her cashmere dress modestly over her knees.

Despite the blinding glare of the studio lights, Vanessa was painfully aware of Nick's presence as she rowed and chatted with customers from all over the country. He'd lingered to watch her make a fool of herself in front of Middle-America.

By the time her replacement arrived, she had developed a megaheadache, but Nick was nowhere in sight when she left the studio complex to drive home.

Upon reaching the house, she felt better, and, seeing Rodney's car in the driveway, she decided to drop in to see if he was settled into the apartment over her garage.

Music was blaring through the open door when Vanessa reached the top of the stairs, and she was smiling when she knocked.

"Come in!" cried a feminine voice.

With a slight lift of one eyebrow, Vanessa went inside. A lovely dark-eyed girl, dressed in blue jeans and a T-shirt, with chocolate-colored hair tumbling to her waist, was sitting in the middle of the living-room floor. She was breaking a thread with her teeth, a tangle of lamé and sequins resting in her lap.

Rodney arrived from the kitchen, carrying two cans of diet pop, just as Vanessa was about to introduce herself. He took over the task with admirable grace. "Van," he said proudly, "this is Gina DeAngelo. Gina, my cousin and landlady, Vanessa Lawrence."

"Hi," Gina said, holding out a hand.

Vanessa was charmed. After returning the greeting, she sank into a chair. "What is that?" she asked, referring to the fabric Gina had been working with.

"It's Rodney's costume," the girl answered, holding up a blue lamé tunic. "He's got a new act. Why don't you show her, Rod?"

Rodney blushed. Despite the fact that he earned his living, as well as his tuition, by working as an exotic dancer, he was shy. "No way," he answered.

Gina let the subject drop, smiling at Vanessa. "You're dating my brother," she said, her brown eyes twinkling.

Vanessa sighed. "I wouldn't exactly say—"

"It bothers her that he used to be a pro athlete, like her first husband," Rodney put in, speaking as though Vanessa weren't there.

Gina shrugged prettily. "To each her own," she said.

Vanessa felt called upon to say something positive about Nick. "Your brother is the most self-assured person I've ever met," she remarked.

Gina shrugged again. "He'd face down the general membership of Hell's Angels without batting an eye," she said, "but let him get sick or hurt himself and he goes to pieces. Last month he cut his finger chopping vegetables for a salad, and you'd have thought there'd been a chainsaw massacre."

Vanessa laughed. It was good to know the idol was human with feet of clay, she thought to herself. But then she remembered his reputation and the parties he was allegedly so famous for and decided he was probably *too* human. Her expression sobered.

"You look so sad," Gina said, exhibiting her brother's propensity for perception. That she could read minds was evident when she went on. "Nick is a really nice man, Vanessa. And he's mellowed out a lot since the old days."

Vanessa was not comforted, nor could she help drawing certain correlations between Nick and Parker. They were both attractive, sought-after men. While finding Parker in bed with another woman had been devastating, she knew that if history repeated itself with Nick, she would be shattered.

Somewhat awkwardly she told Gina that it had been nice to meet her, made an excuse and fled.

As usual, the light on her answering machine was blinking when she let herself into the house. Dreading more of Parker's nonsense, she nonetheless played back the messages.

The first call was from her grandmother, who wanted to know if she and Rodney would be coming to Spokane for Thanksgiving and Christmas that year. The second was from a local television station, where Vanessa had put in an application just before Paul had hired her to be on the Midas Network.

Her heart practically stopped beating, she was so excited. In the middle of Parker's diatribe on how the divorce had been a mistake, she rewound the tape and listened again. She hadn't imagined it; Station WTBE was interviewing potential hosts for a new talk show and they wanted her to come in to see them.

Vanessa had to take three deep breaths before she was steady enough to return the call. When the producer's secretary answered, her voice elevated itself to a squeak.

The secretary was patient. "What did you say your name was again, please?" she asked.

Van closed her eyes, rehearsing her answer. The way things had been going that day, there was every possibility she'd get it wrong. "Vanessa Lawrence," she managed to reply at some length.

"Would a week from Friday be convenient for you?"

Any day would have been convenient, but Van knew better than to make herself sound desperate by saying so. "That would be just fine," she said coolly.

"Two-thirty?" the secretary suggested.

"Two-thirty," Vanessa confirmed, frantically scribbling the date and time on the cover of her telephone book even though the information was emblazoned in her mind for all time.

The moment she'd hung up the receiver, she dashed breathlessly up the rear stairs and into her sparsely furnished bedroom. There, she slid open the closet door and flipped on the light, looking for the perfect outfit, the clothes to convince the producers of *Seattle This Morning* that their search for a host was over.

Soon the bed was piled high with dresses, suits, skirts and blouses—none of which quite met Vanessa's specifications. She had just decided to head for the mall when the telephone rang.

Her cheerful hello brought a burst of blustering frustration from Parker.

"Didn't you get my message?"

"Yes..." Vanessa sighed. "Parker, I don't have time to tango right now, okay? Something really important has come up, and I'm going out."

"You've got a date with DeAngelo, I suppose," Parker immediately retorted. "I could tell you a few things about that son of a—"

The pit of Vanessa's stomach twisted. She wasn't ready to hear the things Parker would say about Nick, not yet. "I've got to run," she interrupted, almost singing the words, "'Bye!"

The telephone started to ring again almost immediately after she'd hung up, and it was still jangling away when she dashed out of the house without turning the answering machine on.

Five hours later she returned with a raw silk suit in a shade of ice blue. There was a Corvette to match sitting behind Rodney's battered sports car in her driveway.

Memories of the way she'd behaved in Nick's apartment combined with a not-so-instant replay of the words they'd exchanged at the studio to make her cheeks hot. The man didn't know the meaning of the word Friday, she fretted. Well, maybe it was just as well that he was there. Now would be as good a time as any to tell him that they shouldn't see each other anymore.

She unlocked the back door, let herself in and waited. Nick was obviously up in Rodney's apartment, passing the time of day. In a matter of minutes he would realize that she was home and appear on some flimsy pretext.

Twenty minutes passed with no sign of Nick. Vanessa had put away her new outfit, changed into jeans and a flannel shirt and even brewed herself a cup of tea when she finally heard an engine roar to life in the driveway.

He was leaving without even saying hello!

Incredulous, Vanessa raced through the house to peer out one of the front windows. Sure enough, Nick was backing the Corvette out into the road, Gina beside him and, as far as Vanessa could tell, he didn't even glance in her direction.

"I'm becoming obsessive," she told the cat, who had come to steer her back toward the kitchen.

Sari made her usual noncommittal comment, and Vanessa gave the animal supper before setting aside her pride and going outside to climb the stairs to Rodney's apartment.

"Hi," he said, looking surprised to see her.

Vanessa took in the very abbreviated cowboy costume he was wearing, raising an eyebrow.

"I was just practicing a new number," he told her, sounding defensive.

His cousin smiled. "Speaking of numbers, I wonder if you'd mind giving me Nick's?"

Rodney eyed her curiously, then shrugged. "Sure, I've got it here somewhere. Are you going to ask him out or what?"

"That's kind of a personal question, isn't it?" Vanessa countered.

"Touchy lady," drawled Rodney as he riffled through his burgeoning address book. "Here it is," he said, scrawling the number onto a piece of scrap paper and holding it out to Vanessa.

She took it, thanked him and left with as much dignity as she could manage.

She gave Nick plenty of time to get home, systematically building up her courage as she waited, and then dialed his number. It was an irony of sorts that she got his answering machine.

The message she left was simple and to the point. "Nick, this is Vanessa. I don't think we should see each other anymore, and that includes dinner on Friday. Goodbye."

It was a long evening for Vanessa, spent with the nervous expectation that Nick would either call or drop by, demanding an explanation for her decision. As it happened, neither the telephone nor the doorbell rang once.

The rest of the week and following weekend was peaceful, too.

On Monday morning, Margie complained about the shadows under Vanessa's eyes as she applied her makeup. "Keep losing sleep like this, kid," the cosmetologist warned, "and you're going to look like Rodney Dangerfield."

Despite everything, Vanessa laughed. "The beginning of another lovely day," she said.

Just then, Oliver Richards dashed in and switched the channel on the monitor from the Midas Network to a popular national talk show. Vanessa stiffened in her chair as she saw the handsome face of her ex-husband fill the screen. She'd forgotten all about Parker's guest spot.

The program had obviously been in progress for a few minutes, and Parker was smiling boyishly at the applause of the predominantly female audience. "I'm happy to say that Van and I are getting back together," he said. "This time I'm going to be the best husband any woman ever had."

The paper cup in Vanessa's hand dropped to the floor, coffee and all.

"Tell us a little about your ex-wife," the program's famous host prompted, watching Parker with a certain speculation in her eyes.

"It's all in the book," Parker answered proudly, and, to Vanessa's abject horror, he held up a copy for the whole world to see.

Vanessa hadn't expected the book to be published for weeks, so her first shock was compounded by a second. "Oh, no!" she cried.

Oliver, standing beside her chair, was wiping Van's coffee from his pants legs with a wad of tissue.

Parker looked directly into the camera, a besotted expression on his face. "I will say this—I love you, Vanessa. And I forgive you for all the times you've . . . hurt me."

Vanessa could bear no more. She lunged for the monitor's Off button and then covered her face with both hands and groaned in helpless despair.

"Congratulations on the reconciliation, Van,"
Oliver boomed. "Does this mean we'll be forced
to get along without you here at the old network?"

Vanessa glared at him, pointedly ignoring his
remark, and stormed out.

That stint on camera was the most difficult of
Vanessa's brief career, and when it was over she
had to sit through a long meeting with the buyers.
The products that would be featured for the next
few days were demonstrated in detail, and price
lists were passed out.

When she got home, the cleaning lady was
there, and the living room was filled to the rafters
with flowers. If Rodney had been around, Vanessa reflected ruefully, he'd have thought he was
back at the funeral parlor.

As she'd expected, the carnations, roses and
daisies were all from Parker, who thought surely
he'd won her heart by forgiving her on national
television. A headache pulsed under Vanessa's left
temple, and she snapped at the cleaning lady when
the doorbell rang.

"Shut that vacuum cleaner off!"

Looking wounded, Marita kicked the switch
and stomped off into the kitchen. Vanessa opened
the door, expecting another shipment of flowers,

and found Nick standing there instead of a delivery man.

His jawline looked like granite. "When did you make the decision not to see me anymore, Vanessa?" he demanded, pushing past her when she didn't invite him inside. "Before or after you came to my apartment and let me make love to you? Before or after you decided to go back to Lawrence?"

Vanessa shoved her hands into her hair. "You didn't make love to me," she said lamely. It was a moot point, but she was desperate. "And I don't have any intention of reconciling with Parker. He made the whole thing up to sell books."

Nick was visibly relieved, but only for a moment. "Just how firm is this decision that we shouldn't see each other again?" he asked quietly, facing her now, standing so close that she could feel the heat and power of his body.

She remembered what Gina had said about the way Nick acted when he was sick or hurt, and a wave of tenderness swept over her. She couldn't help smiling a little. "Why do you ask?" she countered, because she didn't know what to say.

He laid his hands on her shoulders. "Because I'm crazy about you, Value Van."

Vanessa stepped back, lifting one eyebrow. "So crazy that you didn't even return my call when I left that message on your machine. Or was it just that you didn't go home that night?"

Nick sighed. "I went to Portland, Van—I'm opening a new restaurant there."

Marita peered tentatively around the door jamb. She was from some South American country and spoke very little English. "I come back now?" she queried, poised to run.

"Yes," Vanessa said, closing her eyes.

Nick took her elbow gently into his hand. "What do you say we go somewhere and talk?"

Vanessa could only nod, and they'd reached the sensible solace of Nick's apartment before she spoke. "Do you have any aspirin?"

After favoring her with a grin and a kiss on the forehead, Nick disappeared down the hallway, returning momentarily with two white tablets and a glass of water. Vanessa swallowed the aspirin gratefully and then staggered across the room and threw herself down on his cushy sofa.

"The day was really that bad, huh?" Nick said, sitting down on the sofa and placing her feet in his lap. He slipped her shoes off and tossed them away, then began massaging her aching arches and insteps.

"It was terrible!" Vanessa wailed, her arms folded across her face.

Nick went right on rubbing her feet, saying nothing, and she felt compelled to hurl something into the conversational void.

"Why did you leave football?"

Nick chuckled. "I'd made all the money I needed and I wanted to get out before I ruined my back or one of my knees."

The massage felt sinfully good—in fact, it was beginning to arouse Vanessa, though she would never have admitted that. "Sensible," she said with a sigh. "That's you, Nick DeAngelo."

"Um-hmm," he answered, gently working the taut muscles of Vanessa's left calf.

She gave an involuntary whimper. "Stop," she said with such a lack of sincerity that Nick didn't even hesitate.

"Let's go out to the island tonight," he suggested in a reasonable tone.

Vanessa raised her head to look at him. "I have to work tomorrow," she said.

"So do I. There's ferry service—we can be back in plenty of time."

"But we would spend the night?"

Nick didn't look at her. "Yes."

She pulled her leg free and sat up. "I thought we had an understanding about that," she said tautly.

Nick reached out and hauled her easily onto his lap. "I didn't say we'd sleep together," he said in a deep, sleepy voice.

"Then what's the point of going?"

He laughed. "Get your mind out of the gutter, Lawrence. We could walk on the beach, listen to music by the fire and talk. We could play cribbage, drink wine and bake brownies. . . ."

Vanessa rolled her eyes. "You are weird."

"Saturday I was remarkable. What happened?"

Van was feeling harried, and the idea of spending a peaceful night in an island hideaway was not without appeal. But there were those correlations. "I got to thinking that you're probably a whole lot like Parker," she confessed, looking away.

He took her chin in his hand and made her look at him. "I hate it when you do that," he said in a low, angry voice. "Don't compare me to him, Vanessa."

She shrugged. "He's a jock, you're a jock. He's a party animal, you're a party animal—"

"Tell me one thing, Vanessa," Nick interrupted, his dark eyes hot with quiet anger. "Did he let you decide when the two of you would make love for the first time?''

Vanessa looked away. "I don't see what that has to do with anything."

"Did he?" Nick insisted.

"No," she was forced to admit after a long time. Tears welled in her lashes. "No! I had too much wine on our second date and the next morning I woke up in his bed! Are you happy now?"

Nick closed his eyes. "I'm sorry," he said hoarsely.

Vanessa sniffled and started to get off his lap, but his arms tightened around her and the thought of rebelling didn't even cross her mind.

"Are you still in love with him?" he asked.

"No," Vanessa answered without hesitation.

"Then come to the island with me."

"I have a cat to think about, you know," Vanessa pointed out, as Nick began kissing her neck in much the way he had on Saturday.

"Rodney will feed it," he said.

Vanessa trembled. She wasn't ready for a physical relationship, and yet she wondered how she would endure spending a whole night on an island with Nick without offering herself to him.

"Our deal still holds? That I get to choose the time, I mean?"

Nick opened the top button of her blouse. "Yes, but it's only fair to tell you that I'm going to make it hard to wait."

"Oh," Vanessa answered inanely as another button gave way. He slid his hand inside her blouse to caress her breast, and she thought she was going to go insane with wanting him.

As it happened, though, the doorbell rang. Vanessa scrambled to her feet and began righting her blouse while Nick strode, grumbling, across the living room to open the door.

The wonders of the jet age, Vanessa reflected, staring at the visitor in amazement.

Parker glared at Nick as he stepped back to admit him. "It's good to see that you haven't changed, DeAngelo," Parker said furiously.

Nick sighed and ran a hand through his hair. "Is that what you came here to say?" he asked.

Parker had already turned his attention to Vanessa, and he looked for all the world like a betrayed husband, stricken at the discovery of his wife's faithlessness. "How could you, Van?" he rasped. "After the flowers and—"

Vanessa was incensed. "And your generous offer over national television to 'forgive' me?"

"I love you!" Parker bellowed.

"You don't know what love is," Vanessa cried, her chin high and her shoulders square. She took comfort from Nick's presence, but it was even better realizing that she could handle the situation on her own. "Once and for all, Parker, it's over. Now go away and leave me alone."

Parker glowered at Nick, obviously seeing him as the villain of the piece, and then left in a rage, slamming the door behind him.

Vanessa glanced at her watch. "If we're going to the island," she said, "we'd better get started. I need to pick up some of my clothes and feed the cat before we leave."

Nick grinned. "Whatever you say, lady," he teased. "I wouldn't dare cross you."

_____ 5 _____

Nick's island house was gray with white trim and latticework, and it was enormous. Standing hardly more than a stone's throw from the beach, the place had a friendly look about it, and Vanessa's first impression was favorable.

Still, what she knew of Nick's reputation haunted her subconscious, but she refused to entertain the thought. She was tired, even frazzled, and she needed the peace Nick and his grand old house were offering.

The inside was furnished in the same comfortable way as his condominium in Seattle; the sofas and chairs were soft and welcoming, the carpets deep. The paintings were watercolors in muted shades.

Nick led the way through the living room and up the stairway to the second floor. He passed several closed doors, then opened one on the right. "You can sleep in here," he said.

Vanessa bit her lip and slipped past him into a room decorated for a woman. The curtains and the spread on the gleaming brass bed were a pastel floral print, and there were two white wicker chairs in front of the window, their seats upholstered to match.

"It's Gina's," Nick said, laying an index finger to Vanessa's lips just as she was about to open her mouth to ask.

He set her overnight case and garment bag on the bed and gestured toward the hall. "Come on, I'll show you where my room is—just in case."

Vanessa laughed. "Just in case what?"

Nick gave her a look. "Did I forget to tell you? The place is haunted. If you hear anything spooky, all you'll have to do is climb in bed with me and you'll be safe."

"I've heard some lines in my time, buddy," Vanessa replied, preceding him out into the hall, "but that one beats them all."

His room was really more of a suite with a fireplace and six floor-to-ceiling windows that overlooked the sea. Vanessa glanced at the water bed and quickly shifted her eyes away.

Nick shook his head and pushed up the sleeves of his bright turquoise sweater. A look at the half-open door of the closet explained why he hadn't brought spare clothes.

"What we need is some exercise," he said resolutely. "Let's go out for a run before it gets dark."

The way he'd phrased the suggestion made Vanessa feel like an Irish setter, and she did not share Nick's passion for running, but she wanted to be a good sport. She'd brought along an old set of sweats and some sneakers, and she went to put them on.

When she descended, Nick was already downstairs, warming up.

They followed the beach until Vanessa was near collapse, then started back. She knew Nick was adjusting his pace to hers, and she tried not to slow him down too much.

Returning to the house was a vast relief. Vanessa threw herself onto the porch steps, gasping for breath, only to be hauled back to her feet again by Nick. She did seemingly endless cooling-down exercises before he was satisfied that he'd tortured her enough.

"I'm not sure I have the stamina for a relationship with you," she said when they were in the kitchen a few minutes later.

"Why do you think I'm trying to build up your endurance?" Nick got a bag of cookies down from a cupboard and took a carton of milk out of the refrigerator. Sniffing the milk, he made a face and tossed it into the trash.

Vanessa grinned, shaking her head. "Your self-confidence overwhelms me."

Nick took two cookies from the bag and stuffed them into his mouth, one right after the other. "I was hoping it would be my charm and good looks," he said. He was standing right in front of Vanessa before she realized that he'd been approaching her.

She brushed a few chocolate crumbs from his lips. "That, too," she conceded.

Her back was to the counter—that was another fact that had sneaked up on her—and Nick had only to lean against her gently to imprison her. He did that without any apparent attack of conscience, and Vanessa ached in response to the hard grace of his body. He bent his head and kissed her, and his mouth tasted deliciously of chocolate cookies and controlled passion.

Vanessa was dazed when he finally broke away, propelled her toward the back stairway and swatted her playfully on the bottom.

"To the showers, team," he said in a hoarse voice, and when Vanessa looked back over her shoulder, she saw him shove a hand through his hair in frustration.

Since Gina's room didn't come with its own bath like its counterpart in the condominium, Vanessa took her shower in the main bathroom. She put on gray slacks and a kelly green blouse, along with a light touch of makeup.

Nick was dropping an armload of wood onto the hearth in his bedroom when Vanessa finally gathered the nerve to creep to the doorway and look inside. He was wearing jeans and a plaid flannel shirt that he hadn't bothered to button over his T-shirt.

Vanessa cleared her throat to let him know she was there, and he gave her a sidelong grin that said he'd been aware of her presence from the first.

"There's a storm coming in from the north," he said, laying a fire in the grate.

Vanessa's eyes widened, the lightning that had changed her forever still fresh in her mind. Her gaze skittered nervously to the big bed and back again.

Nick saw her trepidation and smiled. "Come in and sit down, Van. You ought to know by now that I'm not going to hurl you down and have my way with you.''

There were comfortably upholstered chairs in front of the fireplace, and Vanessa went to sit in one of them, watching the motions of Nick's back as he finished building the fire, and thinking.

Ever since she'd met Nick, she'd been pondering the powerful effect he had on her senses and emotions, and she understood at least one thing, Nick DeAngelo was the kind of man most women dreamed of meeting—strong, handsome, successful and far too good to be true.

There had to be a glaring fault that would come leaping out at her when she let down her guard and trusted him—and that was the moment Vanessa feared most. She drew her bare feet up onto the chair and wrapped her arms around her legs.

''Tell me about Jenna,'' she said, tilting her head to one side.

Nick sighed and reluctantly turned from the fire. ''Okay. What do you want to know?''

''Why she left you, for one thing.''

''She had a big problem with trust,'' Nick recalled, looking not at Vanessa but beyond her, it seemed, into the distant past. ''I couldn't go anywhere without having her call or drive by to see if I was really where I said I'd be. We started to fight, the marriage fell apart and we went our separate ways."

Vanessa swallowed, remembering her own experience with Parker. "Did you give Jenna reason not to trust you?"

Nick looked insulted that she would even ask the question. "No," he replied with biting directness.

A few moments passed before Vanessa had the courage to speak again. "There was more to it than that, I think," she mused aloud.

"We disagreed about a lot of fundamental things," Nick admitted. "Kids, for instance."

Vanessa sat up straighter. This was a subject that mattered to her. She wanted children of her own more than anything else in the world, including the job on *Seattle This Morning* or a place on a television news team. "She wanted them and you didn't," she blurted out, braced for the worst, expecting Nick to feel as Parker had.

She got another angry, heated look for her trouble. "Wrong," he replied, turning away to throw an unnecessary chunk of wood onto an already thriving fire. "Jenna wanted to be the only child in my life. She was afraid a baby would steal the show."

Vanessa bit her lower lip and looked down at her lap, wishing she'd allowed Nick to tell her what he felt without holding him up against Parker first and then taking her clues from the comparison.

The silence stretched, and Nick finally got to his feet and pushed the screen up close to the fireplace. "What about you?" he asked, keeping his back to her. "Do you want children, Vanessa?"

She swallowed. Here was her chance to distance herself from Nick DeAngelo once and for all, to eliminate him and all the danger he represented from her life. Here was her opportunity to go back to being safe and ordinary.

She couldn't lie to him.

"A houseful," she answered, dropping her eyes when she saw him start to turn toward her.

"What about your career?" he asked. "What about selling foot massagers and wicker birdcages and porch lights?"

He was crouching in front of Vanessa's chair, grasping both its arms in his hands, and there was no way she could escape. "I don't intend to spend the rest of my life selling birdcages and porch lights," she said. "I—I have an interview for another job on Friday, as a matter of fact."

"You're hedging," Nick accused, and the timbre of his voice and the scent of his freshly showered skin combined to make Vanessa slightly dizzy.

"I want to work, Nick," she said quietly, purposefully. "And I want babies, too. When—and if—I remarry, my husband will have to do more than help make children. He'll have to help raise them, too."

"Fair enough," he replied, his voice a husky rumble low in his chest. He drew Vanessa out of her chair, and she ended up kneeling astride his lap.

"Don't we need to go to the store and buy milk or something?" Vanessa queried, her voice an octave higher than usual.

The sound of Nick's laughter seemed to brush against the hollow beneath Vanessa's right ear. "Milk?" he echoed.

"T-to go with the cookies." Vanessa knew she sounded desperate.

He chuckled and began kissing the delicate flesh of her neck. "Cravings already?" he teased.

Vanessa wondered how in the name of heaven she was going to resist this man until she'd reached that mysterious point of readiness that so eluded her. "Nick," she pleaded.

"Hmm?" He pulled out her tucked-in blouse and then proceeded to unbutton it. The tingling pattern his lips painted on her neck continued without interruption.

"This isn't fair," she whispered breathlessly. Her head fell backward as he pushed the front of her blouse aside.

He unfastened the front catch on her lace-trimmed, silky pink bra, freeing her. "Life is never fair," he reminded her.

Against her better judgment, Vanessa leaned back even farther when his hands rose to cup her breasts. "Ooooooh," she said.

Nick was kissing his way down over her collarbone. "My sentiments exactly," he replied just before he closed his mouth over one straining nipple.

Vanessa clasped both hands behind her head, increasing both her vulnerability and her pleasure. Her lips were parted, and her eyes closed as she reveled in nurturing Nick; she could feel and hear his desire, and it heightened her own.

He was moaning as he enjoyed her like a man wild with fever, and when she would have lowered her hands, he held them in place. The fingers of his left hand rubbed Vanessa's bare back, at once positioning her for his own unrestricted access and stroking her reassuringly.

The moment he released her wrists, Vanessa was peeling off his shirt and tossing it away, tearing at the T-shirt beneath. She would have undressed him completely if his position hadn't made that impossible.

His chest was muscular and matted with dark hair and, as Vanessa had, he leaned back slightly, in effect surrendering at least a part of his body to her explorations. He gave a powerful shudder and moaned low in his throat as she kissed, caressed and nibbled at him.

After a long time he rose gracefully to his feet, drawing Vanessa with him, clasping her close even as he stripped her of her blouse and dangling bra and began unfastening her slacks.

"If you want to stop this, Vanessa," he warned, "turn around and walk out of the room right now. Whatever self-control I might have had is gone, and all bets are off."

Looking up into his smoldering brown eyes, Vanessa remained where she was and opened the top button of his jeans. "All bets are off," she repeated, to let him know that she understood what was about to happen, that she welcomed it.

He kissed her then with all the passion he'd been holding back, and Vanessa could only guess at the strength it had taken to restrain such a torrent. She was hardly aware of being carried to the bed or undressed, and even though the sky outside was clear and quiet, the room crackled with lightning.

Nick was poised above her, his mouth covering hers in another mind-splintering kiss, the mattress rippling sensuously beneath her. Vanessa ran gentle hands up and down his broad, sinewy back, telling him without words that she wanted him.

He took her in a long, slow thrust that set her to twisting her head from side to side on the pillow, delirious in her need.

"Easy," he rasped out, and she could feel the struggle between Nick's mind and his body as he lay perfectly still inside her. "Take it easy, sweetheart. We have all the time in the world. . . ."

Vanessa tried to force him to provide the friction, the motion, that she needed so desperately, but he was too big and too powerful and she could not move him. "Oh God, Nick. Why do you do this to me—why do you love making me wait?"

He chuckled and gave her a single, searing stroke metered to drive her insane, but his expression was serious when he spoke. "I want you to remember this always—it has to be special."

Vanessa arched her neck, felt his lips descend to the fevered skin there. "It is—I swear it. I'll remember..."

His laugh vibrated through his vocal cords and captured her heart like a warm summer wind. "So this is the secret to making you agree to my terms, is it?" he teased.

But he began to move upon her after that, quickening his pace heartbeat by heartbeat, stroke by stroke until Vanessa was covered from head to foot in a fine sheen of perspiration, until she was moaning and flinging her head from side to side.

"Let go," Nick whispered raggedly near her ear. "Stop fighting it and let go." His words broke down the last flimsy wall enclosing Vanessa's soul.

With a series of straining cries, she surrendered all that she was to Nick, all that she'd ever been or ever would be. The relief was exquisite; for a time, her soul escaped its bonds and flew free.

There was no restraint in Nick's release. He trembled, lunged deep inside her and cried out in satisfaction as pleasure induced its unique seizure.

For a long time afterward there were no sounds in the room except for their breathing and the popping of the fire. Then inexplicably, uncontrollably, Vanessa began to weep.

Nick groaned and rolled over to look down into her face. "Don't do this to me, Van," he pleaded, wiping away a tear with one thumb. "Please, don't be sorry for what we did."

She shook her head. "I'm not," she managed to say. "It's just that—"

He kissed her briefly on the mouth. "It's just that we don't know each other well enough, right?"

She nodded. "Right."

He leered at her and wriggled his eyebrows. "Okay, I'm an eighties guy, I can relate. What's your sign, Baby?"

Vanessa gave a shout of laughter through her tears. "Stop," she pleaded. "This is a sensitive moment."

Nick squinted at the clock on the bedside stand. "It's also dinnertime, and I'm hungry as hell. Let's make spaghetti."

Vanessa was too relaxed to contemplate getting up and doing any kind of work. "Make spaghetti? I *am* spaghetti."

"I have a hot tub," Nick wheedled, sliding downward and beginning to kiss her neck again.

Vanessa knew where that would lead. She twisted free and sat up. "You have a hot tub," she mused, looking at Nick with shining eyes. "What the devil does that have to do with cooking spaghetti?''

Nick declined to answer that and said instead, "On second thought, let's go out to dinner. I don't want you to get the idea that I'm a cheap date."

They took a shower, this time sharing the same stall, and dressed in the clothes that had been strewn from one side of the bedroom to the other. Vanessa reapplied her makeup and styled her hair.

"I hope this place is casual," she said, giving Nick's jeans and flannel shirt a look.

The restaurant was a few miles away on the edge of the only town the small island boasted, and the spaghetti there was good.

"The owner must be Italian," Vanessa guessed, stabbing a meatball with her fork and lifting it to her mouth.

"Paddy O'Shaughnessy?" Nick teased. "Definitely. He probably grew up in Naples, or maybe Verona."

It was a night full of nonsense, restorative and precious, and Vanessa didn't want it to end. She knew, of course, that it would, and that the morning would bring painful regrets. She concentrated on enjoying Nick, the spaghetti and, later, the hot tub.

There were plants in the glass-walled room where the hot tub bubbled and churned, and Vanessa wrapped herself in the night sky with its glittering mantle of stars. "This must be what it's like when you're on safari," she said after swallowing a sip of wine. "I can just imagine that we're camped alongside a steaming river with crocodiles slipping by, unseen, unheard . . ."

"Now that's a romantic thought," Nick observed.

Vanessa hiccuped and looked accusingly at her wine. "I've had too much *vino*," she told Nick seriously. "I'd better sleep in Gina's bed tonight."

If Nick was disappointed, he didn't show it. "Whatever you say, princess," he said quietly, taking the glass from her hand and setting it on the tiled edge of the large square tub. "I don't want you to have any regrets when you look back on today."

"I won't," Vanessa said, even though she knew she would. The wounds Parker had left were only partially healed, and she wouldn't be able to disregard the similarities between him and Nick forever.

When she yawned, Nick lifted her out of the tub. "Time for bed," he said. "We have to get up early."

Vanessa scrambled for a towel, not because she was naked, but because she was chilled, and she watched unabashedly while Nick got out of the tub and switched off the jets. He was so incredibly secure in his masculinity that he didn't reveal the slightest qualm about being nude.

When he pulled on a blue terrycloth robe, it was an unhurried action, meant for comfort and not modesty. In fact, when Vanessa came to him he opened the garment long enough to enfold her inside, against his ribs.

They walked upstairs that way, talking idly of spaghetti and hot tubs, and parted after a brief kiss in the doorway of Gina's room.

The sheets were cold. The moon and stars must have all gathered on the other side of the house, for there was no light for Vanessa to dream by. She missed Nick, even though they had parted only a few minutes before and he was just one room away.

Snuggling down determinedly, she closed her eyes and commanded herself to sleep. Despite her utter weariness, oblivion eluded her. She tossed, turned and tossed again.

Finally she got out of bed, put a robe on over her striped silk pajamas and padded across the hall.

"Nick?" she questioned softly from the doorway of his room.

He sounded sleepy. "What?"

"I think I heard something."

A motion in the moon-shadowed bed and a throaty groan of contentment told her he was stretching like some cocky panther. "Like what?" he asked innocently.

Vanessa shrugged. "You said there were ghosts...."

"Yup," Nick agreed, "I did." He threw back the covers to make a place for her beside him. "There's only one thing to do, Tonto. Circle up the wagons and share a bunk."

Vanessa was across the room and between Nick's satin sheets in a wink. She snuggled up against him, reveling in his warmth and his strength. "I'm going to hate myself when I wake up in the morning," she confessed with a contented sigh.

Nick kissed her forehead. "I know," he answered sadly. "And me, too, probably."

Vanessa rested her head on his shoulder. "Probably," she said, and then she dropped off to sleep.

When she awakened at dawn, Nick was gone. She knew he was probably out running, and she was grateful for the time to sort out where she was and what she'd done the night before.

She'd had her shower and dressed for work by the time Nick returned. Clad in running shorts, a tank top and a jacket, despite the fact that November was fast approaching, he looked at Van warily as he crossed the kitchen. He opened the refrigerator and took out the milk he and Vanessa had stopped for on the way home from O'Shaughnessy's the night before.

"Let's hear it," he started. "You hate me, you had too much wine last night and waking up the morning in my bed was an instant replay of the first time with Parker. Right?"

Vanessa was eating a slice of whole wheat toast slathered with honey. "Do I look traumatized?" she asked, chewing.

He cocked his head to one side, frowning. "No," he said, sounding surprised. "Are you saying you don't regret letting me make love to you?"

"Excuse me," Vanessa said, pouring herself a cup of the coffee that had been waiting when she came downstairs, "but you didn't do everything, you know. I was half of that little encounter." She paused and drew a deep breath, then let it out. "To answer your question, yes and no."

Nick gave her a wry look. "Yes and no. I like a decisive woman."

"It was too soon," she said. "I probably wasn't ready."

He set the milk back in the refrigerator and put his hands on his hips. "You seemed ready to me," he replied.

Vanessa blushed at the good-natured jibe and sipped her coffee to avoid having to say something.

"That takes care of the yes. What about the no? What don't you regret, Vanessa?"

Vanessa dropped her eyes. "The passion," she answered after a long time. "You brought me back into the world, Nick, and I'm grateful."

"Gratitude isn't exactly what I had in mind, but it'll do for now," he answered, and then he disappeared up the stairs. When he came back, he was wearing tan corduroy slacks, gleaming leather boots and a green turtleneck sweater.

Vanessa assessed him appreciatively. "How much time have we got before the ferry leaves?"

Nick took in her blue suede dress and sighed heavily. "Not enough," he lamented. He took her in his arms and kissed her with knee-weakening thoroughness before whispering hoarsely, "I wish we could stay here forever."

Vanessa laid her head against his chest. "Me, too," she said, but she knew the magic was already slipping away.

It seemed sadly fitting that, when they drove aboard the ferry to return to Seattle, dark clouds were gathering in the northern sky.

The storm Nick had predicted was almost upon them.

6

When Vanessa finished her segment that morning, Parker was waiting at the door of the women's dressing room. His arms were folded across his chest, and his features were set in a sour scowl.

"Where were you last night?" he demanded in a furious whisper.

Vanessa sighed. "We're divorced, Parker, and that's all I'm going to say about last night or anything else." She started to walk around him, but he reached out and took her arm in a painful grasp.

His nose was an inch from Vanessa's as he rasped, "You slept with him, didn't you?"

Vanessa wrenched free of his hold, her face hot with color. A receptionist was approaching with a folded piece of paper in her hand, looking scared.

"Sh-should I call security, Ms. Lawrence?"

Vanessa saw nothing to fear and everything to pity in Parker's eyes at that moment, and she shook her head as he made a visible effort to control himself. "Everything is fine, Karen," she lied.

Karen darted an uneasy glance at Parker and held out the paper to Vanessa. "Mr. DeAngelo called while you were on the air," she explained.

Vanessa scanned the note and suppressed a sigh. There was some kind of problem at the new restaurant in Portland, and Nick would be away until Friday. She bit her lower lip and crumpled the message into a ball. "Thank you," she said to the receptionist, who promptly hurried away.

"Have lunch with me," Parker said.

Vanessa stared at him. "You must be insane."

He treated her to his most endearing smile. "Look at it this way—if you don't, I'll just follow you home and you'll have to feed me anyway."

"I'd be more likely to call the police," Vanessa said.

Parker shrugged. "Whereas a restaurant would be a safe, neutral place—very public."

Vanessa sighed. She was in a glum mood and Parker was the last person she wanted to spend time with, especially when she knew he was going to tell her something she didn't want to know, but she finally nodded. She couldn't hide forever.

While her ex-husband waited, she toned down her makeup, gathered up the list of times she would be selling the next day and braced herself for the worst.

A soft rain was falling as Parker and Vanessa hurried across the employee parking lot to her car. Parker had arrived in a cab, which said a lot about his confidence in his powers of persuasion.

Unable to stand it any longer, Vanessa looked at him out of the corner of her eye as she snapped her seat belt into place. "You're going to tell me something about Nick, aren't you? Something awful."

Parker's expression was one of regretful gallantry. "This thing between you and him is getting serious, and I can't let it go any further."

"What?" Vanessa cried, frustrated beyond all bearing. "What's so terrible about Nick?"

Parker sighed. "All I'm going to say for right now is that he's not husband material. DeAngelo is ten times the bastard I ever was."

Vanessa offered no comment on that, and as she drove out of the studio compound, she gnawed nervously at her lower lip. Normally she wouldn't have given Parker's words any credence—he was, after all, a lying, manipulative cheat. But she had a spooky, gut-level feeling that this time he had something valid to say.

"Where do you want to go for lunch?" she asked even though every trace of her appetite was gone.

He named a nearby bar and grill, and Vanessa drove toward it.

They were settled in a booth with cushioned leather seats and roast beef sandwiches and glasses of beer in front of them, when Parker grinned at her and said, "Just like old times, huh, Van?"

Vanessa rolled her eyes. "Stop it, Parker. Too much has happened for us to be sitting here pretending to have fond memories."

Parker looked hurt. "You don't have any happy memories of us? Not even one?"

Vanessa thought of the early part of their marriage when she'd adored Parker, when everything he said had made her either laugh or cry. She'd lived on an emotional seesaw in those days, believing herself to be happy. In retrospect, she knew she had suffered. "Don't push, okay?" she said, averting her eyes. She hadn't been able to touch her sandwich, but she reached for the glass of beer with a trembling hand.

"You're really nervous, aren't you?" Parker's features darkened, indicating an approaching storm. "Are you that crazy about DeAngelo?"

Vanessa saw no point in lying. "Yes," she said straight out. "I am."

"Why?" Parker demanded, and some of the shaved beef slid out of his sandwich because he was squeezing it so hard.

Vanessa shrugged, trying to look nonchalant even though her stomach was roiling and her throat was closed tight. It wasn't fair of her to try to convict the man she loved on whatever it was Parker was going to say, especially when Nick wasn't there to defend himself.

"This is a mistake," she blurted, sliding across the bench to stand and shrug into her coat. "I shouldn't have come here—"

"Vanessa, sit down," Parker said, and something in his tone made her meet his gaze.

Her courage failed at what she saw there, and she dropped back into the seat, covering her face with both hands for a moment and sighing. "Tell me, Parker. Stop playing games and say it."

"He's using you to repay me for something that happened a couple of years ago."

The statement sounded so preposterous that Vanessa almost laughed out loud. Almost. "Like what?"

Parker sighed heavily and, for just a second or so, he looked honestly reluctant. "Did he mention Jenna—his ex-wife?"

Vanessa nodded. "Yes."

The expression in Parker's blue eyes was distant and vaguely arrogant. "What did he tell you about the divorce?"

Powerful forces battled within Vanessa, one faction wanting to stay and hear Parker out, the other clamoring for escape. "He said she had a problem with trusting him, and that she didn't want to have children."

Parker shook his head, as though marveling at some tacky wonder. Then, without further ado, he dropped the bomb. "She and I had an affair, Vanessa. Nick caught us together and he's been out to get me ever since."

For a moment the words just loomed between Vanessa and Parker, quivering with portent. Then they exploded in Vanessa's spirit, and tears of pain filled her eyes. She put a hand to her throat and rose shakily to her feet.

"Tell me it's a lie, Parker."

He shrugged and, incredibly, reached for his sandwich. "I'd like to, babe, but I can't. The truth will out, and all that."

Vanessa turned and stumbled toward the door. The storm had come and rain was pounding on the sidewalk as she stood in the cold wind, heedless and broken. She walked slowly to the car, her hands trembling so that it took several attempts to get the key into the lock and open the door.

When she was inside, she let her forehead rest against the steering wheel and drew deep breaths until the desire to scream had abated a little. She was just fitting the key into the ignition when the door on the passenger side opened, and Parker flopped into the seat, sopping wet.

"You shouldn't be alone right now," he said somehow managing to look as though he really gave a damn.

"Get out," Vanessa said. She was soaked to the skin, her hair was dripping rainwater and she knew her mascara was running down her face in dark streaks. She didn't care about any of those things. She wanted to be alone; she needed it.

Parker actually had the gall to reach out and grip her hand. "It's okay, Van—I'm going to take care of you. You'll forget about DeAngelo in no time."

Vanessa was cold and her teeth were beginning to chatter. "Get out," she said again, and after a second's hesitation Parker left the car, slamming the door behind him.

She drove home by rote, tears streaming down her face, and she hadn't had time to pull herself together before Rodney appeared. He let himself in through the kitchen door, took Vanessa by the shoulders and pressed her into a chair.

"Good God," he breathed, "you look awful! What happened? Did somebody die?"

Vanessa nodded. "Me," she answered. "I died, Rodney—fifteen minutes ago in Toddy's Bar and Grill."

Rodney put a hand to her forehead and then went to the cupboard for a mug. He promptly filled it with water and shoved it into the microwave. While it was heating, he plundered the cabinets until he found Vanessa's fruitcake brandy.

When he'd made a cup of instant coffee liberally laced with brandy, he set it on the table in front of Vanessa and sat down in the chair beside hers. "Talk to me," he said quietly.

Vanessa reached for the mug, holding it in both hands, letting it warm her fingers. "I can't," she said. "Not yet."

The door opened, and Gina slipped in. "Is everything okay?" she asked.

Vanessa averted her eyes, humiliated. She didn't want Gina to go to her brother and report that he'd broken her. His plan of revenge had succeeded beyond his wildest expectations.

"It's got to be about Nick," Rodney mused.

A strangled sob escaped Vanessa.

Gina spoke softly to Rodney. "I'd better go. I'll call you later."

"Sure," Rodney replied with affection, and he kissed Gina's forehead before she left the house.

Vanessa took a steadying sip of the brandied coffee.

"So," Rodney said, dropping back into his chair at the table, "tell me about the murder of Vanessa Lawrence back there at Toddy's Bar and Grill."

Vanessa shook her head. "Not now."

"Okay," her cousin said, "if you won't talk, at least go upstairs and get out of those wet clothes before you catch pneumonia."

Thinking of the important interview scheduled for Friday, Vanessa nodded woodenly. "Okay." She got up and walked up the stairs, stiff and slow of movement, carrying her coffee with her. She took a brief hot shower, then put on flannel pajamas and collapsed on her bed.

"You love Nick that much, huh?" Rodney asked from the doorway. He'd brought another cup of coffee, probably doctored, and he proceeded toward Vanessa's bedside.

She took the cup. "That's ridiculous. I've only known him a few days." And in that short length of time he had recreated her world.

Rodney sat down on the foot of the bed since Parker hadn't left any of the chairs when he moved out. "Why do I get the feeling that your ex-husband had something to do with this?"

Vanessa set her coffee on the bedside table and wriggled under the covers. "Nick's been using me," she said, ignoring her cousin's question. "God, Rodney, what an actor he is—you should have seen him!"

"What did Parker tell you?" Rodney persisted.

"That he had an affair with Jenna DeAngelo and Nick caught them together," she said, and a new wave of pain washed over her as she said the words out loud.

"And you bought that?" Rodney bit off each word, clearly annoyed. "Van, you know Parker would rather climb the tallest tree and lie than stand flat-footed on the ground and tell the truth!"

Their grandfather had said those very words right after Van had introduced Parker to him. She wished she could be in Spokane now and be held in the old man's strong, gentle arms. "What Parker said was true," she said sadly. "I can't explain how I know, but I do."

Rodney rolled his eyes. "Great. You're not even going to give Nick a chance to tell his side of the story, are you?"

The mention of his name went through her like a lance. As soon as Rodney left, she would roll herself into a fetal ball and die. "He used me to get back at Parker," she said miserably. "Now go away and leave me alone. I'm terminal."

Rodney gave the telephone beside her bed a pointed glance. "I'll be in my apartment if you need me," he told her, and then he was gone.

Vanessa drank the rest of her coffee with brandy and slipped under the covers to wait for the hurting to stop. It followed her relentlessly, even into her sleep.

She awakened hours later, when the room was glowing with moonlight, to find Nick sitting on the side of the bed, looking down at her. She started to pull the covers over her head, but he caught her wrists in an inescapable grasp and held them on either side of the pillow.

"What are you doing in my house?" she spat, struggling, to no real avail, against the hands that imprisoned her with such gentle effectiveness. "Get out, and don't ever come back!"

Even in the half darkness she saw the pain in Nick's eyes. God, how calm and collected he was. He should have been the one to work in the broadcasting business, not her.

He spoke in a steady, though hoarse, voice. "I'm here because Gina called me and told me you were in pieces. Rodney filled me in on the rest."

"It's true, isn't it?" Vanessa ventured to ask, looking at him with wide eyes.

Nick sighed and released her hands. He shoved splayed fingers through his rain-dampened hair. "Part of it. I did come home one night and found Jenna and Parker together."

Vanessa felt herself breaking apart inside. "And you swore revenge?"

"Hardly. I beat the hell out of him and left. He didn't tell you that part of the story, though, did he?"

"You lied to me," Vanessa accused. "You used me to get back at him!"

"I didn't care enough about Jenna to do that, Vanessa," Nick replied, still avoiding her eyes. "In one sense, I was actually relieved that it was finally over between us."

"You're glossing over the fact that you wanted revenge."

"I told you," Nick said with cold patience, "I had all the vengeance I wanted that night. Can you say you don't remember a night when your devoted husband came home with a few cuts and bruises?"

Vanessa shuddered. She remembered all right. Parker had claimed he'd been mugged, but refused to report the incident to the police. He and Vanessa had been married a little over six months at the time. "My God," she whispered.

Nick reached out to touch her face, and she slapped his hand away.

With a sigh, he got up and walked over to one of the windows that overlooked the street. "I think we'd better stop seeing each other for a while," he said after a long time.

Vanessa was stunned and infuriated. If anybody was going to break off this relationship, it was going to be her. She was the one who had been wronged!

She threw back the covers and struggled out of bed. "Wait just a minute, Nick DeAngelo!" she shouted, waving her finger at him.

Instantly he was facing her, and his face was taut with fury. "Listen to me," he ground out. "I won't play these games, Vanessa. I'll be damned if I'll involve myself with another woman who refuses to trust me!"

Vanessa's mouth dropped open.

"Goodbye," Nick said bluntly, and then he walked out, leaving her standing there, in the middle of her bedroom, feeling even worse than she had before.

Throughout the rest of the week, Vanessa functioned like an automaton. She got up in the mornings, fed the cat, got dressed and went to work. When that was done, she went home, fed the cat again and crawled into bed, usually without supper.

By Friday, the day of her interview, she looked less than her best. Wearing some compound Margie had given her to cover the shadows under her eyes, she presented herself at WTBE-TV in her new raw silk suit.

The front she put on must have been effective because the interview went very well. Although the program wouldn't actually go into production until after the first of the year, she was informed, the final decision would be made before Thanksgiving. Would she be able to leave Midas Network by the middle of December?

Vanessa answered yes, thanked the woman who had interviewed her and left. Some fundamental instinct told her she was going to get the job. She still wanted it very much, but the excitement was gone.

Since Nick had walked out of her bedroom three days before, so many things had stopped mattering.

She glanced at her watch and saw that it was three-fifteen. She'd promised to meet Janet Harmon for a drink, so she set out for the Olympic Four Seasons at a very reluctant pace.

Janet would probably grill her about the breakup with Nick, and Vanessa didn't want to burst into tears in the bar of a swanky hotel.

Sure enough, her friend looked grimly determined when Vanessa met her in the elegant lobby.

"Paul and I stayed here on our wedding night," she said to make conversation, but it was plain that Janet's mind wasn't on her own relationship. "How did the job interview go?"

"I think they're going to hire me," Vanessa answered dispiritedly as they entered the cocktail lounge and seated themselves.

"Paul will be beside himself," Janet answered, "and not with joy, either."

Vanessa sighed and averted her eyes for a moment. "Stop pretending you didn't ask me here to find out what happened between Nick and me," she said.

Janet, a pretty woman with shoulder-length dark hair and blue eyes, folded her arms on the table top and leaned forward slightly. "I don't have to ask, Vanessa—I already know. Paul is Nick's best friend, remember?"

A waitress came, took their orders and left again.

"I'd be very interested to hear Nick's side of the story," Vanessa said stiffly.

"Then why don't you go over to DeAngelo's after you leave here and ask him to tell it to you?" Janet replied in clipped tones.

"Oh, great," Vanessa complained. "You're mad at me, too!"

"I'm furious. Nick DeAngelo is the best thing that's ever happened to you, and you're not even going to fight for him."

The waitress returned, setting a glass of white chablis in front of Vanessa. Janet was having a martini, and she made a small ceremony of eating the olive.

At any other time Vanessa would have been amused. As it was, she just wanted to go home, feed the cat and slink back into bed. To get it over with, she said, "I admit it. I was going to break off with Nick, and he beat me to the punch."

"He's a wreck," Janet informed her. "Paul says he's never seen Nick so low."

Vanessa took a certain satisfaction in knowing she wasn't the only one suffering. She lifted her wineglass to her mouth and sipped the chablis before answering, "He'll get over it, and so will I."

"I don't understand this," Janet pressed. "You fell in love with Nick the first night you met him— I know because I was there and I saw it happen. And now you're just going to walk away without looking back?"

"I'm not going to crawl to him," Vanessa said firmly. "I still think he used me to get back at Parker and I despise him for it."

"You don't know Nick very well." Janet sighed, sounding resigned at last. "He'd never do a thing like that. He's too open, and he hates games and little intrigues."

"He also hates me," Vanessa said, remembering the look in his eyes when he'd told her goodbye. "Let's drop the subject, please, because if we don't, I'm going to fall apart right here."

Janet must have believed her because she didn't mention Nick's name again. The two women finished their drinks and parted, vowing to meet for lunch before the holidays got into full swing and there was no time.

It was four-thirty when Vanessa got home—too early to go to bed and hide from her depression. She changed into jeans and a Seahawks T-shirt, fed Sari and proceeded to the living room, which was still choked with Parker's flowers.

She dropped one fading bouquet after another into a large plastic garbage bag and carried it out to the curb, where Rodney had already set the trash for morning pickup. She was stuffing the bag into one of the plastic cans when an ice-blue Corvette slipped sleekly into her driveway and Nick got out.

He looked as bad as she felt.

"Hi," he said, rounding the car to stand beside Vanessa and effectively block any retreat to the house.

Even though she'd rehearsed this moment through a thousand varying versions, she wasn't prepared to face Nick. She averted her eyes and said nothing at all.

Nick sighed, and out of the corner of her eye she saw him wedge his hands into the hip pockets of his jeans. "Damn it, Van, will you at least listen to me? I'm willing to admit I was wrong—I should have told you about Parker and Jenna."

"Why didn't you?" Vanessa asked, raising wary, pain-filled eyes to his face.

His formidable shoulders moved in a shrug. "It was water under the bridge to me. I didn't think it mattered."

Vanessa bit her lower lip. "You don't want to be involved with a woman who doesn't trust you—remember?"

Nick swore under his breath. "And you still don't, right?"

Vanessa sighed. "When you've been married to a man like Parker, it doesn't come easy."

"Speak of the devil," Nick marveled as a cab swept up to the curb and Parker got out.

He probably wouldn't have been so brave if he hadn't had another man with him. "That's the idea, Van," her ex-husband said, smiling as he approached, "Toss DeAngelo out with the trash and get on with your life."

Parker's friend, a yuppie-type wearing a three-piece suit, looked at him as though he'd gone mad.

Nick favored Parker with a slow, leisurely grin. "Keep talking," he said. "Right now I'd like nothing better than stuffing you into one of these cans and stomping you down like a milk carton."

Parker paled a little beneath his health-club tan, but he recovered his aplomb quickly enough. "Vanessa," he said, evidently choosing to pretend that Nick wasn't there, "this is Harold Barker. You're getting a second chance, baby."

Vanessa folded her arms, unconsciously protecting herself. "At what?" she asked in suspicious tones.

Parker looked enormously pleased with himself as he explained that Harold was the executive producer of yet another nationally syndicated talk show. "They want you to go on with me next week and help pitch the book."

The idea was born in a rebellious area of Vanessa's mind. She cast a sidelong look at Nick before saying expansively to Parker and Harold, "Come in, come in. This sounds like an interesting proposition."

Nick muttered another swearword, joining them even though Vanessa had made a point of not inviting him.

"Did you want something, Mr. DeAngelo?" she asked coolly when the four of them were standing in her half-furnished living room.

Nick gave her a look that would have made a vampire cower, planted himself in front of the fireplace and folded his arms across his chest. He was clearly staying for the duration, and that pleased Vanessa, even though she felt a conflicting desire to march over there and kick him in the shins.

Over a drink, solicitously served by a doting hostess, Harold explained his concept of a show including both Parker and Vanessa. He was sure the viewing audience would enjoy hearing her reactions to the things her ex-husband had written about her.

"Of course," he finished, casting a nervous glance toward Nick, "we'll want to discuss your—er—reconciliation with Mr. Lawrence, too."

Vanessa beamed, perching behind Parker on the back of one of the two easy chairs he'd left her and ruffling his hair. "It's a romantic story," she said, well aware that Nick was seething even though she didn't dare look at him.

Parker was obviously baffled, but his tremendous ego served him well in his hour of need. He swelled up like a peacock and then shrugged in that aw-shucks-folks way that had made him such a hit with the fans. "I guess we were just swept away by passion," he said.

At last Vanessa risked a glance in Nick's direction. It was obvious from his grin that he was on to her game, even if Parker and Harold weren't.

Vanessa was still looking at Nick when she responded to Parker's remark. "It was incredible," she said.

7

"It's Friday night," Nick said stubbornly, standing in Vanessa's kitchen with his arms folded. "We had a date, remember?"

Vanessa sighed. It was dark outside, even though it was still early, and there was a wintry chill in the air. She took her old sweater from the peg inside the pantry door and put it on. "We can't just go on as though nothing happened, Nick," she reasoned, wishing they could do exactly that.

"Because you still don't trust me," he ventured to guess.

She gently bit her lower lip for a moment. "I want to, but you're so much like Parker...."

His eyes darkened. "I didn't come over here to be insulted," he informed her. "Furthermore, damn it, I'm nothing like that bastard!"

Vanessa took a can of vegetable-beef soup from the cupboard. Since the argument with Nick, she'd been virtually living on the stuff. "You are," she insisted. When he started to speak, she held up a hand, palm outward, to silence him. "Besides the pro-athletics aspect, there's your reputation. Do you deny that you're known far and wide as a rounder and a ladies' man?"

Nick jerked the soup can out of her hand, stuck it up against the can opener and pushed down on the handle so that an angry whir filled the kitchen. "Who the hell told you that?" he demanded. "Parker?"

Vanessa shook her head, reclaiming the soup, dumping it into a saucepan and adding water. "I'm not sure where I heard it. I just know, that's all." She studied him pensively as she put the mixture on the stove to heat. "You know, I think it's very interesting that Jenna didn't trust you when she was the one who was fooling around. Was yours an open marriage, Nick?"

He rolled his eyes, looking more annoyed by the moment. "Not on my end, it wasn't. As for Jenna, her own guilty conscience made her suspect me."

"Want some soup?" Vanessa asked, getting two bowls down from the shelf even as she spoke because she knew he wasn't about to leave.

Nick sighed. "No, but I'll eat it," he answered. While Vanessa was stirring the broth, he called DeAngelo's and instructed someone to send over two orders of clam linguine and a bottle of white wine.

She was grinning when she brought the steaming bowls of soup to the table. "A man of sweeping power and influence," she commented, as much to keep the conversation moving as anything.

Nick was frowning as he sat down. "How did your job interview go?" he asked.

"They're going to hire me, I think," she answered, reaching for a basket of saltine crackers she'd set out earlier and squashing a handful into her soup. "Of course, if they see me on national television with Parker, they may change their minds."

For a few moments, Nick said nothing. He was busy adding crackers to his soup. When he finally spoke, his tone was serious. "You're really going to do that? I thought you were just stringing Parker along to get rid of him."

Vanessa swallowed. "Yes, I'm really going to do that," she confirmed. "And I'm pretty sure he'll stop being a problem from then on."

"What about us, Vanessa?" Nick wanted to know, and there was a vulnerability in his voice that made her love him all the more hopelessly. "Where do we go from here?"

Inside Vanessa ached. She knew there could be no relationship without trust, and as much as she longed for things to be different, she hadn't reached the point where she could let herself rely on any man's integrity. She looked away, unable to answer.

He reached out and took her hand in his. "Okay, babe. So be it. I'll back off for a while."

The prospect made Vanessa's world seem as dark as deep space. "Don't you dare leave me here to eat two orders of linguine all by myself," she warned, on the verge of tears.

He smiled sadly and stayed, but Vanessa was conscious of the vast distance between them—one that might never be bridged.

Presently he found another subject, seemingly a safe one, and asked, "How did you get into telemarketing?"

It was a relief to think about something besides her own mixed-up emotions, doubts and fears. "I majored in broadcast journalism in college," she said. "Parker insisted that I drop out when we got married. He was traveling all the time, and I didn't have much to do once the house was clean and everything, so I started looking for work.'' She paused and lowered her head for just a moment, then went on. ''Janet Harmon has been my friend for a long time. When the Midas Network came to Seattle and Paul was hired as production manager, he gave me a job.''

''Selling gold chains and answering machines to the masses,'' Nick remarked, setting his empty soup bowl aside and regarding Vanessa with puzzled eyes, ''is a far cry from broadcast journalism.''

She was instantly defensive. ''Some of us don't just fall into our dream jobs and become instantly successful,'' she pointed out tartly. ''I had to take what I could get.''

The doorbell chimed in the distance like the ringing of the gong between rounds of a boxing match. Nick must have deemed it a good time to retreat to his own corner, for he slid back his chair and disappeared toward the front of the house.

Vanessa hastily rinsed out their soup bowls and put them into the dishwasher, wondering what would happen between her and Nick and how it would be if he did indeed back off for a while.

She had a feeling that life would become as dull a chore as cleaning out an oven or stripping years of wax from a linoleum floor.

When Nick returned he was carrying a sizable white bag and a bottle of wine. Plundering the cupboards and drawers, he brought forth plates, silverware and a pair of dusty wineglasses.

Vanessa immediately took the glasses from him and carried them to the sink, where she washed them in hot soapy water while Nick set out the meal he'd had sent over from his restaurant.

"This house reminds me of your life," he observed when she finally rejoined him at the table and took up her fork to eat linguine. "Lots of empty spaces."

She glared at him as she chewed the most exquisite pasta she'd ever tasted.

He opened the wine bottle and poured chablis into her glass. "Well?" he prompted, arching one dark eyebrow. "Aren't you even going to fight back?"

"No," Vanessa responded after a few moments of tight-jawed deliberation. "If you want to be a jackass, that's your prerogative. I don't have to jump on the proverbial bandwagon and become one, too."

Nick grinned at her, more in amazement than good humor, and shook his head. "At least you're not denying that there are some gaps that need filling. I guess that's progress."

Although Vanessa was furious, she managed to keep her temper under control. "Thank you for your analysis. And to think some people actually pay psychiatrists when all they'd need to do is ask the great Nick DeAngelo to tell them how to run their lives!"

He sighed, and the sound conveyed an infinite sadness. "It isn't going to work, is it?" he asked, setting down his fork and leaning back in his chair.

A massive, hurtful lump formed in Vanessa's throat. She closed her eyes for a moment, then shook her head. "I don't think so," she said.

Nick stood, taking his leather jacket from a peg on the wall and shrugging into it. "I know it sounds crazy," he said hoarsely, keeping his back to her, "but I love you, Vanessa. When and if that ever means anything to you, call me."

With that, he opened the back door and went out.

Vanessa sat still in her chair for a long time, stunned and utterly confused. Then she got up and scraped the remains of their dinner down the garbage disposal, taking grim satisfaction in grinding it up. She just wished that she could throw in her memories of Nick as well to be pulverized and washed down the drain.

Trying to sleep proved to be a useless effort that night. At the first glimmer of dawn, she called Nick.

He answered on the second ring, sounding wide awake and quietly desolate.

"How could you tell me you love me and then just walk out like that?" Vanessa asked.

"Who is this?" he countered, and she could practically see his wonderful, dark eyes dancing with mischief.

Vanessa laughed miserably. "Damn it, Nick, don't make this any more difficult than it already is."

He sighed. "The whole thing is pretty confusing to me, too, if that makes you feel any better."

"It doesn't."

"You made the call, Vanessa," Nick pointed out. "The ball's in your court."

She shoved a hand through sleep-tangled auburn hair, then bit down on her thumb nail. "I'm in love with you," she finally admitted.

"That's progress," he conceded, but he still sounded the way Vanessa felt—sad.

She closed her eyes against an ocean of scalding tears. "What I'm trying to say, I guess, is that I need some time."

"Fine," he retorted. "How does a hundred years strike you?"

"That was mean!"

Nick was silent for a few moments, and when he went on his voice was low and ragged. "I've told you before," he explained with a slow patience that was patently insulting, "I don't play games. If I can't be totally committed to this relationship, I don't want any part of it."

Vanessa felt as though he'd slapped her. "I see," she said.

"Should you ever feel ready to take the risk, get in touch with me. If I'm not involved with someone else, we'll see what happens."

Outrage replaced shock. "Of all the arrogant—"

"I'm through shadowboxing with you, Vanessa. I want a wife and a family and I'm not going to wait forever."

"How dare you threaten me that way!"

"It isn't a threat," Nick answered, his words grating together like rusty nails in the bottom of a bucket. "It's a fact."

"Goodbye," Vanessa said after a brief interval.

He hung up without returning her farewell.

Vanessa was determined not to fall apart again. She was a modern woman, she told herself, independent with a career. She didn't need Nick DeAngelo to be whole.

Oh, but she wanted him. She wanted him.

When a few hours had passed and she'd recovered her composure to some degree, she dialed the Harmons' number. Paul answered.

Vanessa explained that she had some personal business to take care of and asked for a few days off.

"Are your grandparents all right?" her employer asked, his voice full of concern.

At the mere mention of them, Vanessa ached with homesickness. She would have given a lot to be back in Spokane, pouring out her heart to the people who had raised her, but there wasn't going to be time for that. "They're fine," she answered belatedly, feeling strangely tongue-tied. "It's—it's something else."

Paul sighed. "All right," he said in his kind and quiet way. "Take as much time as you need."

"Thanks," Vanessa replied. She asked Paul to give her best to Janet and then hung up.

She had finished packing and was just carrying her suitcase downstairs when Rodney arrived to check up on her.

"I saw Nick's car here last night," he said, standing in the doorway to the kitchen and eying the suitcase. "I guess the two of you are going away together for a few days, huh?"

Again, Vanessa felt a hollowness inside. "Wishful thinking, Rod," she answered in resigned tones. "I'm flying to New York with Parker."

Seeing Rodney's mouth fall open was the only fun Vanessa had had in days. "What?" he croaked.

Vanessa smiled. "He's been pestering me to tell the world what I think of his book, and that's what I plan to do," she said.

Rodney's eyes rounded, and a grin broke over his face as her meaning struck him. "Wow," he breathed. "He'll kill you."

"He'll want to," Vanessa agreed, and just then the doorbell rang.

"I'll get it," Rodney volunteered, loping toward the front door. Even though he was in his second year of chiropractic school, there were times when he was still the gawky boy Vanessa remembered.

She stood up a little straighter when she heard him talking to Parker. Since there was no love lost between the two men, the exchange was terse.

Seeing Vanessa, Parker smiled fondly as though there had been no ugly divorce and then kissed her cheek. "You are as lovely as ever," he said.

Vanessa thought of something teenagers had said when Rodney was in high school. *Gag me with a spoon.* "Thank you, Parker," she said aloud. "So are you."

He gave her a bewildered look and then glanced at his Rolex.

You'd think a man who could afford a watch like that would at least let his ex-wife keep all the furniture, Vanessa reflected.

"Let's go," Parker boomed in sunny, all-hail-the-conquering-hero tones. "We've got a plane to catch. Thought we'd have dinner at Tavern on the Green."

Why not? Vanessa thought. *He's paying.* "Sure," she enthused. A cloud passed overhead as she considered potential problems. "You did book separate rooms, didn't you, Parker?"

He cleared his throat and looked away for a moment. "Thanks to my publisher, we have a penthouse suite. Nothing but the best for you, darlin'."

She arched one eyebrow as they started toward the door, but didn't pursue the point. They could agree on sleeping arrangements later. "You'll feed Sari until I get home and bring in the mail?" she asked of Rodney, who lingered in the entryway, watching her and Parker with a worried expression in his eyes.

He nodded. "Sure."

Some impulse made her hurry back and plant a kiss on Rodney's cheek. *Don't worry,* she mouthed before turning back to Parker.

There was a taxi waiting at the curb, and Parker made a great show of squiring Vanessa to it and sweeping open the door. She almost—not quite, but almost—felt guilty for what she was going to do to him.

They were at the airport, about to board their plane, when Nick suddenly appeared, moving gracefully through the crowds of travelers as he approached. Vanessa felt a lump of dread rise in her throat and averted her eyes momentarily.

Parker was cocky, shoving his hands into the pockets of his tailored trousers and rocking back on the heels of his Italian leather shoes. "I thought you had more pride than this, DeAngelo," he dared to say.

Vanessa gave her ex-husband a wild look and elbowed him, but when she turned her amber eyes to Nick, she was smiling.

"What is it?" she asked sweetly.

Nick took her arm in his hand and pulled her around a pillar, his nose an inch from hers. "You're not actually going through with this, are you?" he demanded in a sandpapery whisper.

She widened her eyes, well aware that Parker, while feigning arrogant disinterest, was actually listening. "I have to," she answered. "Thank you for coming to see me off and goodbye!"

"Goodbye, hell," Nick rasped. "I have half a mind to buy a ticket on this plane and go to New York with you. Wouldn't that be romantic—just you, me and your ex-husband."

Vanessa drew in a deep breath, then let it out in a hiss. It was a technique she'd learned once in a relaxation seminar. "Go away." She smiled. "Please?"

Nick bent around the pillar to glare at Parker. "Are you going to sleep with that rat?" he demanded.

"Talk about a lack of trust," Vanessa pointed out, lifting her chin.

Nick closed his eyes for a moment. "You're right," he admitted at length. "I shouldn't have asked you that."

They were calling for the first-class passengers to board the plane, and Vanessa had to leave.

She told him the name of the hotel where she would be staying, adding, "I'll call you as soon as I'm settled."

But Nick shook his head. "I'll be in Portland. We'll talk when you get home."

Vanessa stood on tiptoe to kiss him lightly on the mouth, and Parker took her arm and dragged her away toward the boarding gate.

She was feeling a confused sort of hope when she and her ex-husband were settled in their seats, the coach passengers trailing past them into the body of the airplane.

Some of them recognized Parker and clogged the aisles, asking for autographs, but Vanessa paid little attention to them. She was staring out at the terminal, wondering what Nick was thinking.

For the first time, she allowed herself to hope that things might eventually be all right between them, once she'd dealt with Parker and his book. That would close one chapter of her life, and she'd be able to begin another.

Parker spent most of the trip flirting with a particularly attractive flight attendant; it was only when they had landed at JFK that he turned his efforts back to Vanessa.

A long silver limousine had been sent to fetch them, and Vanessa smiled as she settled into the suede-covered seat. She meant to enjoy every possible luxury while she could since she would undoubtedly leave town on a rail, covered in tar and pigeon feathers.

Twilight was falling as they drove toward the hotel, and Vanessa gazed out through the tinted windows, drinking in the spectacle of light and the cacophony that is New York.

Twice she had to pull her hand out of Parker's fingers. She began to regret the act she'd put on a couple of days before.

"This trip is strictly business," she whispered, hoping the driver wouldn't hear. "So keep your hands to yourself, Parker Lawrence!"

Parker looked wounded. "How are we going to reconcile if I can't touch you?" he inquired.

Vanessa was tired and hungry and she was beginning to have serious doubts about the wisdom of this venture. "We're not going to get back together ever, and you damned well know it," she said irritably.

She glanced in Parker's direction and saw that he was watching her with a disturbing sort of shrewdness in his blue eyes. "Then why did you come with me?" he asked.

Vanessa sighed. Maybe she should just forget her plan and go home—by way of Portland. The deception seemed too big to carry off now. "I wanted to come to New York," she hedged.

Parker didn't speak to her again until they'd reached their hotel, which overlooked Central Park, and checked in.

The suite was spacious with a breathtaking view of the city and it came equipped with its own bar—and even a glistening black grand piano. There were flowers everywhere, compliments of Parker's publisher, and a bottle of Dom Perignon was cooling in a bed of ice.

Vanessa made sure there were two bedrooms and that hers had a lock on the door before taking off her coat and unpacking the few clothes she'd brought with her.

She changed into a navy silk shirtwaist for dinner and saw a familiar light in Parker's eyes when she returned to the suite's living room. He was standing by the piano and, grinning, he ran one hand over the keyboard, filling the place with a discordant exclamation.

There was a pop as a waiter opened the champagne. After accepting a tip from Parker, the whip-thin young man—an aspiring dancer, no doubt—slipped out of the suite.

Once again, Vanessa had misgivings. In fact, she wished she'd run after Nick at the airport and made him take her to Portland with him. Her yearning for his voice, his smile, his touch, was an ache deep within her.

"You look troubled," Parker observed, his eyes discerning. "What is it, Vanessa?"

She wrung her hands together and drew upon all her courage. The idea that had seemed so just and so wise had turned foolish somewhere along the line. Even infantile. "I was going to humiliate you, Parker," she confessed. "I meant to denounce your book on that talk show tomorrow and tell the whole world what a lie it is."

To her surprise, Parker threw back his handsome head and laughed. "Your innocence never ceases to amaze me, Vanessa," he crowed when he'd recovered a little. "Do you think I didn't know that from the first?"

Vanessa's mouth dropped open.

Suavely Parker poured champagne into a crystal glass and extended it to his ex-wife. "Friends?" he said, his voice a throaty rumble.

Vanessa accepted the glass, took an unseemly gulp of its contents and retreated a step, her eyes still wide. She was confused about almost everything in that moment, but one thing was clear as the icicles that lined the eaves of her grandparents' house every winter: Parker had no interest in being her friend.

"Why are you staring at me that way?" he pressed, tilting his head to one side and looking ingeniously baffled.

She finished off her champagne and ignored the question. "Let's go to dinner. I'm starved."

Parker consulted his watch. "Our reservations are for an hour from now, but I guess we could have a few drinks while we wait." Even though the restaurant was within walking distance, he went to the telephone and summoned the limousine.

Vanessa didn't question the gesture, reasoning that people didn't go into Central Park on foot at night if they could avoid it, but her mind and heart were far away as one of the hotel's elevators whisked them to the ground floor.

Tavern on the Green was an oasis of lighted windows in the darkness, and Vanessa felt more at ease when she and Parker were settled inside with cocktails and a candle in a jar between them.

"You're still seeing DeAngelo," Parker speculated flatly, and Vanessa was amazed to realize that he'd restrained himself from asking that question for most of the day. Patience wasn't his long suit.

"Yes and no," Vanessa said, her throat hurting. She wondered what Nick would say if she caught a plane to the west coast, took a cab to the restaurant in Portland and surprised him.

"What do you mean 'yes and no'?" Parker demanded. "Damn it, I hate it when you do that!"

Vanessa could be charitable, thinking of how Nick would welcome her. They'd probably go somewhere private, right away, and make love for hours. "We're trying to negotiate some kind of workable agreement," she said.

"You make it sound like a summit meeting," Parker grumbled, looking like a disgruntled little boy. "Doesn't it matter that he was using you?"

Vanessa took a sip of her drink, a fruity mixture that barely tasted of liquor. She was so hungry that she was beginning to feel a bit dizzy. "I'm not sure he was," she said. She looked at her ex-husband pensively, champagne and the cocktail mingling ominously in her system. "He swears he's nothing like you, and sometimes I believe him."

Parker looked roundly insulted. "Am I that terrible?" he demanded.

"You're not a man I'd want to have a lasting relationship with," Vanessa answered with a hiccup.

"Good Lord," Parker grumbled, squinting at her. "You're drunk!"

"I am not," Vanessa protested.

Just then a flash went off, blinding her. For one awful moment, she thought the Soviets had pushed the button. Then she realized that some reporter had recognized baseball's very own bad boy.

For once, Parker didn't look pleased at being noticed. "Get out of here," he said to the hapless person-of-the-press, glaring.

The reporter took another picture before two waiters came and discreetly evicted him from the premises.

"We're very sorry for the annoyance, Mr. Lawrence," a man in a tuxedo came to say. "Your table is ready."

Vanessa was wildly grateful at the prospect of eating. Light-headed, she staggered slightly when she rose too quickly from her chair, and Parker had to steady her by putting an arm around her waist.

Dinner must have been delicious, although Vanessa was never able to recall exactly what it was. She knew only that she consumed it with dispatch and then ordered dessert.

When they reached the hotel, there was a party going on in the suite. Vanessa skirted the room full of laughing, smoking, drinking strangers to let herself into her private chamber and lock the door.

The message light was blinking on the telephone, and she smiled as she rang up the desk. Nick had called about an hour before and left a number in Portland.

She punched out the digits with an eager finger, and when Nick said hello, Vanessa replied with a hiccup and a drunken giggle.

8

"Put Parker on the line," Nick said, sounding irritated.

Vanessa raised three fingertips to her mouth to stifle another hiccup. "You left a message because you wanted to talk to Parker?" she asked, bitterly disappointed.

An exasperated silence followed, and then Nick swore. Completely ignoring her question, he posed one of his own. "How much have you had to drink, Vanessa?"

A hiccup escaped. "Too much," Vanessa admitted. The noise outside her room seemed to be getting louder with every passing moment, and she was developing a headache. "There's some kind of party going on in the living room," she observed out loud.

"Get Parker," Nick reiterated in an ominously quiet voice.

With a sigh, Vanessa laid the receiver on her bedside table and ventured into the next room, weaving her way through the happy revelers until she finally came to Parker.

"Nick wants to talk to you on the telephone," she said.

Parker grinned and touched her cheek, as though she'd brought him good news. "Fine," he replied, and started off toward the nearest extension.

Nick was speaking when Vanessa got back to her room and picked up the receiver again.

"If you take advantage of her, Lawrence," he warned, "what happened two years ago will be nothing compared to what I'll do to you this time."

"The lady made her choice," Parker replied smoothly, no doubt drawing courage from the fact that Nick was on the opposite coast. "She came to New York with me, and she's staying in my suite. If you can't pick up on the meaning of that, maybe you'd better go back to hawking cod at the fish market."

Vanessa sucked in a breath, horrified and furious. They were discussing her as though she were a half-wit, unable to look after herself or make her own decisions. "Wait a minute, both of you!" she cried, her headache intensifying as the music and laughter got louder in the living room. "It just so happens that I have a thing or two to say about all this!"

"Whatever, darlin'," Parker said in a bored tone, and then he hung up. His confidence in his own powers of seduction was an affront Vanessa would not soon forgive.

"Nick," she said, "don't you dare hang up."

"I'm here," he answered, a sort of broken resignation in his tone.

"None of this is at all the way it sounds. I have my own room, even if it is in Parker's suite, and there's no way he and I are going to get back together. Understood?"

Nick gave a ragged sigh. She knew intuitively that he was remembering what she'd told him about her first time with Parker—that she'd had too much wine and woke up in his bed.

"I don't have any claim on you, Vanessa," he said at last. "You can do what you want."

While Nick's words were perfectly true, they were not the ones Vanessa had hoped to hear. She wished devoutly that she'd listened to him and stayed in Seattle, where she belonged.

Vanessa sat up a little straighter on the edge of the bed, thinking of all the women who probably chased after Nick whenever the opportunity presented itself. "Are you telling me that you think we should both see other people?"

Nick made a grumbling sound of frustration and weariness. "Is that what you want?" he retorted.

Vanessa closed her eyes. "No," she admitted.

"Good," Nick replied. "When are you coming home?"

"Monday," Vanessa vowed. The door of her room opened, and a woman wearing a leather jumpsuit and a white lamé wig peered in. "I'm sorry, this room is private," she told the intruder.

The woman mouthed an oops and slipped out, closing the door behind her.

"What the hell was that all about?" Nick demanded.

"You'd never believe it," Vanessa replied, yawning. "Shall I just go to Seattle, or make it Portland?"

Nick was quiet for a moment. "Portland. But you have the show to tape tomorrow, don't you?"

Vanessa held her breath briefly in an effort to put down another attack of the hiccups. "I'm not staying for that," she said. "I realize now that all my protests will do is make more people rush out and buy the book."

He chuckled, and the sound was warm and low and so masculine that Vanessa ached to be close to Nick. "Speaking of the book, there are a few things I'd like to know about the incident in Chapter Three," he said.

Vanessa sighed. "A circus acrobat couldn't do that," she replied.

Nick laughed outright. "I love you," he said.

She hiccuped again.

"Strange that he didn't write about your drinking problem," Nick teased.

"Good night, Mr. DeAngelo," Vanessa said with feigned primness. "I'll see you in Portland sometime tomorrow."

"Make sure I know the flight number, and I'll pick you up."

Vanessa nodded, her mind fuzzy, and then remembered that Nick couldn't see her. "Okay. And Nick?"

"What?"

"I love you, too."

"Good night, sweetheart," he said, and his voice was a caress.

After hanging up, Vanessa went immediately to her bedroom door and locked it. Then, after laying out the trim royal blue suit she planned to wear on the flight home the next day, she slipped into her private bathroom and took a long, soothing bath.

When she returned to her room, sleepy and comfortable in her favorite pair of flannel pajamas, Parker was sitting on the end of her bed and the party was still going on full blast in the living room.

"What are you doing here?" she demanded in a furious whisper, pulling on her robe and tying the belt tightly. "How did you get in?"

Parker held up a key. "Relax, Vanessa—for all my sins, I've never forced myself on you, have I?"

Vanessa had to admit that he hadn't though sometimes his methods had been almost that lowdown. She shook her head, still keeping her distance.

"You're not going to do the show tomorrow, are you?" Parker asked, sounding resigned.

"No," she answered. "Are you angry?"

Parker sighed. "It might be to your advantage to go on and show the world that you're not a drunk," he announced.

"A what?" Vanessa demanded, her eyes rounding. With Nick the reference had been a joke, but Parker was coming from a different place altogether.

"You remember that reporter at the restaurant tonight, I'm sure—the one with the blinding flash attachment on his camera? He's from the *National Snoop*, and your delightful face will be propped up beside every checkout counter in America within a week to ten days." He drew in a deep breath and let it out again, his eyes narrowed in speculation. "I can see the headlines now: TOSS-AWAY BRIDE DROWNS HER SORROWS, it will say—or something to that effect."

Vanessa felt the color drain from her cheeks. She had a career of her own to think about, and she couldn't afford publicity of that kind. No one would ever take her seriously if she were seen in such an unflattering light.

"Go on the show tomorrow, Van," Parker said quietly, coming to her and taking her hand in his to pat it. "Show the world who you really are."

Vanessa wrenched free of his grasp. "You don't give a damn what the public thinks of me," she hissed, "so spare me the performance. All you care about is selling that rotten book of yours!"

Parker shrugged. "The choice is yours, Vanessa. Go or stay."

She thought of Nick waiting for her in Portland and imagined how it would be to be held in his arms again, to lie beside him in the darkness as he quietly set her senses on fire. She closed her eyes for a moment, torn.

"I'll stay," she said, averting her eyes.

"Um-hmm," Parker agreed smugly, and then he tossed Vanessa the key to her room, went out and closed the door.

She promptly locked it, then hurried back to the telephone, planning to call Nick and explain that she'd changed her mind about doing the talk show with Parker.

As it happened, though, Vanessa set the receiver back in its cradle without pushing the sequence of buttons that would connect her with Nick. She couldn't explain the situation to him when she didn't completely understand it herself.

There was no time to call the next morning because a limousine arrived to collect Parker and Vanessa at an ungodly hour. She rode to the studio in a daze, sipping bitter coffee from a Styrofoam cup.

She promised herself that she would call Nick as soon as she had a chance, but it seemed that the talk show people had every moment planned. The instant they arrived, Vanessa was whisked away to have her makeup redone and her hair styled.

As the cosmeticians worked their wonders, a production assistant briefed her on the structure of the show and the line the host's questioning would probably follow.

None of it was anything like Vanessa expected. In fact, when she and Parker were seated before an eager audience and the lights flared on, all her broadcasting experience seemed to slip away into a parallel universe. It was as though she had never appeared before a camera in her life.

To make matters worse, she had slept very badly the night before, and she probably looked like someone who should be sent away for the cure.

The audience, mostly female, was clearly interested in Parker. It was amazing, Vanessa reflected, how the man could flirt with so many women at once.

Numbly Vanessa groped her way through the hour. She answered the questions presented by the host and the audience as best she could and was grateful when the program ended.

Vanessa fled the studio immediately afterward, caught a cab outside and sped back to the hotel. There, she picked up her suitcase and went straight to the airport.

She had to wait three hours for a flight to Portland, and that was routed through Denver and San

Francisco with a long layover at each stop. She called Nick from Colorado and told him that she would be in at six that evening.

He didn't sound particularly enthusiastic, and Vanessa could only assume that he'd watched the show, seen her sitting there as stiff as a wooden Indian, letting Parker display her like a sideshow freak.

A glum, drizzling rain was falling when Vanessa reached Portland, but the moment she saw Nick, her spirits lifted. Although he gave her a rueful look and shook his head at some private marvel, he took her in his arms and held her close, and that made up for a great many things.

"I've had a terrible day," she said, letting her cheek rest against the front of his cool, rain-beaded leather jacket.

He kissed her forehead. "I know," he replied gruffly, and then he put an arm around her waist and ushered her toward the baggage claim area.

After reclaiming Vanessa's suitcase, they went outside and Nick hailed a cab. All the way to his restaurant, they made small talk, avoiding the issues of Parker and her appearance on television. There were long, stiff gaps between their sentences.

"You're angry with me," Vanessa said when the cab had stopped in front of a towering Victorian building with a view of the water and an elegantly scripted sign that read, *DeAngelo's*.

Nick paid the driver and waited until the cab had pulled away before answering, "Does it matter, Vanessa?"

She sank her teeth into her lower lip. "Yes," she said, after they'd mounted the steps and entered the interior of the restaurant. "Of course it matters."

Wonderful aromas greeted Vanessa, reawakening her appetite.

Nick gave her a look. "Whatever you say," he replied, putting his hand to her back and propelling her toward a set of sweeping, carpeted stairs.

Vanessa decided to save the serious issues they needed to talk about for later when she'd had some aspirin and something to eat. "Do you stay right here at the restaurant when you're in Portland?" she asked, trying for a smile.

He nodded, opening a pair of double doors to admit her to an office that was the size of some hotel suites. "Sit down and relax," he ordered, setting down her suitcase and striding toward the telephone on his desk. "I'll have some dinner sent up. What do you want?"

"Spaghetti," Vanessa answered without hesitation, thinking of the night in the San Juan Islands.

Nick nodded again and placed the order in clipped, brusque tones. It was obvious that he was distracted.

"I thought you weren't going to be on the talk show," he said, when the silence had lengthened to its limits.

So he'd seen the debacle. Vanessa lowered her eyes, embarrassed that she'd been so tongue-tied on the program. Everyone who'd watched—and the producers of *Seattle This Morning* might well have been among them—was probably thinking that she had all the personality of a secondhand dishrag.

"I changed my mind," she replied almost in a whisper.

Nick sighed. "That was your prerogative," he replied. "You're here, and that's all that matters."

Vanessa looked at him with wide, weary eyes full of relief. "You were right," she conceded in a small voice. "I shouldn't have gone. I only made things worse."

Nick crossed the room to sit beside her, and the moment he took her into his arms she burst into tears.

He kissed her eyelids and her wet, salty cheeks before taking her mouth and taming it with his own. Vanessa's exhausted body was captured in an instant and largely involuntary response, and she gave a strangled moan when he lifted one hand to caress her breast.

"The spaghetti will be here in a few minutes," Nick muttered against the warm flesh of her neck.

Vanessa laughed even as she tilted her head back in pagan enjoyment of his attentions. "You're so romantic, DeAngelo."

He drew away from her very reluctantly and shoved one hand through his hair. "You'd better reserve judgment on that, lady," he warned.

A sweet tingle went through Vanessa, but she was cool and composed as she arched an eyebrow and queried, "Until when?"

"Until I take you to bed, which will be about sixty seconds after you finish your spaghetti."

Vanessa looked around. "You have a bed here? This is an office!"

Nick pointed toward a closed door on the other side of the room, but said nothing.

She felt her temper flare. "How convenient," she said, folding her arms.

Nick sighed, shook his head and grinned at her. "We party animals like to be prepared," he said.

Vanessa honestly tried, but she couldn't sustain her anger. She was too tired and she wanted him too badly. "Don't tease me," she pleaded.

He touched her nipple and, even through her blouse, it came instantly to attention. "No promises," he said just as a knock sounded at the door.

The spaghetti had arrived, but there was no wine. Diet cola was served instead and Vanessa, who was seated at the small table in front of the windows, gave Nick a knowing glance while the waiter poured it for her.

"Are you afraid I'll lose control of myself?" she asked the moment they were alone again.

"Afraid? Hardly," Nick said, folding his arms and watching as Vanessa ate. "I'm looking forward to it, if you must know."

Vanessa blushed. She did tend to shed her inhibitions when Nick made love to her. "I'm serious, Nick," she said.

"So am I," he replied.

Vanessa tried not to gobble down her spaghetti, but there was no hiding the fact that she was eager to be taken to Nick's bed and driven beyond her own restraints. He was grinning at her when she dabbed hastily at her mouth with the napkin and shoved her empty plate away.

"Go ahead and—er—get settled. I'll be in in a few minutes."

Vanessa was possessed of such virginly shyness all of a sudden that she couldn't even look at Nick. She picked up her suitcase.

Those few steps toward the door he'd pointed out earlier seemed to take half an hour to execute, and when she was finally out of his view, she sagged with relief.

The room was not as large as his suite on the island, but it was full of Nick's personality and his scent, and Vanessa felt at home there. With a sigh, she sat down on the edge of a brass bed covered with an old-fashioned patchwork quilt and kicked off her high-heeled shoes. It had been a long day.

In the adjoining bathroom, Vanessa took a hot, hasty shower, then put on tap pants and a camisole. She brushed her teeth and misted herself with cologne, and when she returned to the bedroom Nick was there, waiting for her.

"I missed you so much," she confessed, her chin at a proud angle.

"And I missed you," he answered gruffly, making no move to approach her.

Vanessa knew she would have to go to him this time, but now that they were alone and she was ready for him, it didn't matter. She crossed the shadowy room, which was lit only by the stray glimmers of street lamps outside, and slid her arms around his lean waist.

"Love me, Nick," she whispered, looking up at him, knowing her whole soul showed in her eyes and not caring. "I've been fantasizing about you so much that I'm going to go crazy if you don't touch me."

He cupped his strong hands on either side of her head, stroking her satiny cheeks with the edges of his thumbs. After searching her face with his dark, smoldering eyes for several seconds—as though to commit every feature to memory—he bent his head and kissed her.

His seductive kiss was a gentle kind of mastery, and Vanessa swayed as Nick gave her a foretaste of the fiery conquering she knew he would make her earn.

When he finally broke away, it was only to slide her embossed white camisole over her head and toss it into a chair. Her breasts seemed to swell, filling with a nectar meant only for him, as he admired them.

Vanessa's knees went weak when he reached out to weigh her bounty in one hand, the pad of his thumb preparing the nipple to nurture him. She wanted to lie down and abandon herself to Nick, but he wouldn't allow that. He put his free arm around her waist to support her, and she bent backward by instinct, silently offering herself.

With a groan, Nick bent to taste the nipple he'd already taught to obey him. His hand moved away, sliding down over Vanessa's ribcage to the place where her waist dipped inward to tug at the waistband of her tap pants.

She trembled as she felt the last silken barrier give way, cried out softly when he caressed her. The excitement was building steadily, and Vanessa didn't want it to be over so soon.

"Stop," she pleaded, her head bent back as Nick fed greedily at her breast. With his hand he taught her new levels of pleasure. First he beckoned, then he soothed, now he taunted. "Oh, Nick, please—please—I'm going to..." There was a fierce explosion inside Vanessa, and her hips convulsed as Nick extracted every trace of response from her.

She was still gasping for breath, still so bedazzled that she could barely see when he laid her gently on the bed and began taking off his own clothes. When he was naked, Nick joined her.

Although most of the tension had left her body, Vanessa gave herself up gladly to the slow, skillful massage Nick treated her to. She caught the scent of some fragrant oil, felt it seeping into her skin as he applied it with circling motions of his fingertips.

Finally he could no longer restrain himself from her breasts and, with a groan, he found a nipple and drank of Vanessa until she was writhing in need. She asked Nick to take her, but he only turned her onto her stomach and repeated the process with the oil.

Vanessa was in an odd state of mingled excitement and sweet satiety, and the thrumming need inside her increased until she couldn't wait any longer. She twisted onto her back again and gasped a fevered plea.

Her hands moved over Nick's chest, his back, his buttocks in a wild, soft urging, and finally, blessedly, his resistance snapped. He took her in a hot, sweeping stroke that made her cry out in welcome and arch her back to receive him as completely as possible.

Her name was a ragged rasp torn from his throat, and though his mouth dipped to hers in an attempt at a kiss, he was too frantic to linger. With a desolate groan, he began quickening his pace by degrees until Vanessa's hips were rising to meet his.

His magnificent head was tilted back in triumph and surrender as he strained, visibly, to prolong the sweet anguish that consumed them both. Finally with a growl of lust he joined Vanessa in the core of a flaming nova. Even when their bodies parted much later, their souls remained fused together.

Vanessa was the first to recover, and she gave Nick a teasing kiss on the belly before sitting up and moving to slide off the bed.

"Don't go," he said, taking her wrist in a painless grasp and holding on.

She allowed him to pull her back down beside him, to kiss and caress her until the treacherous heat was building inside her again. In this second joining, there was no control on either of their parts, no withholding from the other and no teasing. It was fast and it was primitive, and when it was over Vanessa didn't even try to leave the bed because she couldn't move.

She awakened in the depths of the night to find herself alone, and an incomprehensible, unfounded dread forced her heart into her throat.

"Nick?" she called, getting up and groping for her robe.

She found him in the adjoining office, half dressed and sound asleep in his desk chair.

Full of love and relief, Vanessa went to him and laid her hands on his shoulders. "Nick?" she said again.

He woke with a start and pulled her deftly onto his lap. "Hi," he greeted her with a rummy yawn.

Vanessa kissed his forehead. "Come back to bed," she said.

He gave another yawn. "This reminds me of page 72," he said.

"Page 72?" Vanessa echoed, completely puzzled.

Nick pulled a copy of Parker's book from underneath a stack of papers and held it two inches from her nose.

Vanessa snatched the volume from his hand and flipped through it until she'd found the page in question. Hot color pooled in her cheeks as she read, and her eyes grew wider with every passing word. She'd forgotten this passage.

"I never did any such thing!" she cried, slamming the book closed and flinging it away.

Nick smiled wickedly. "Are you against trying it?" he teased.

Vanessa laughed, her anger fading. "Wretch," she said, giving him a quick kiss on the mouth and a push to the chest, both at the same time.

He rose out of the chair, forcing Vanessa to stand, too, and gave her a little shove toward the bedroom.

There, Vanessa undressed Nick after shedding her robe, but there was no more lovemaking that night. They slept, legs and arms entangled, heads touching.

The moment she opened her eyes in the morning, however, all Vanessa's doubts and fears were back, lined up at the foot of the bed like an invisible army. This time she sent them packing, determined to enjoy her time with Nick. Things were still far from settled between them, and she didn't want to waste a moment.

He was singing in the shower and she joined him under the spray, although she was nowhere near as brave in the daylight as she had been in darkness.

Nick greeted her with a resounding kiss, then proceeded to lather every inch of her body. The water ran cold long before they came out.

9

Until that day, Vanessa's impression had been that Nick dabbled at running his restaurants since he obviously didn't need to earn a living. By noon she knew he worked the same way he made love—with a quiet, thorough steadiness neither hell nor high water could deflect him from.

Watching him fascinated Vanessa, but it also made her restless. She had her own fish to fry, and her thoughts began turning in the direction of Seattle, the Midas Network and the decision being made at WTBE-TV. Leaving Nick in the middle of a loud argument with the chef, she went upstairs where there was privacy and silence and reached for the telephone to punch in the numbers that would cause her answering machine to play back any accumulated messages.

Her eyes widened as she listened. Representatives of six different stations, in that many different cities, had called with requests to "discuss" her career plans. Parker had left word that he'd realized he loved Darla after all and was off to Mexico to be married, and the cleaning lady had imparted that she was going to quit if Vanessa didn't buy a new vacuum cleaner.

When Nick entered the room a few minutes after the messages had ended, Vanessa was still sitting on the corner of his desk with the receiver in one hand, staring off into space.

He frowned as he hung up the telephone and peered into her eyes. "Is everything all right?" he asked.

Dazed, Vanessa nodded. "Parker is getting married and my housekeeper is going to quit," she said.

Nick put a hand under her chin. "You can always get another housekeeper," he said, looking worried.

Vanessa realized that he thought she was shattered by the news of her ex-husband's remarriage, and she laughed. She wanted to reassure him. "I'm glad Parker is tying the knot, Nick," she said truthfully. "Now maybe he'll leave me alone."

"Your eyes are glazed," Nick insisted. "If it isn't unrequited love, what's making you look like that?"

She told him about the messages from the six television stations. "I have to go home, Nick," she finished, resting her hands lightly on his shoulders.

He sighed, and while he didn't seem threatened by her news, he wasn't pleased, either. "You can call them from here, can't you?"

She shook her head.

Nick looked toward the window for a few moments, but Vanessa knew he wasn't seeing the glum weather or the modern skyline. "None of those stations are in Seattle?"

Again, Vanessa shook her head.

He kissed her lightly on the lips. "I've got to stay here until I can replace this chef," he said reluctantly.

Vanessa felt bereft inside, as though some great chasm had opened between them, and maybe it had. She called the airport and made a reservation on a flight leaving in an hour, then hastily packed her clothes.

Nick offered to see her off, but she declined, needing time and space to think about the future and the unexpected changes it might bring.

Sari greeted her with an annoyed *reoooww* when she arrived home, but was appeased by an early supper. Vanessa returned the calls on her answering machine in a methodical and professional fashion.

Her appearance on national television, far from ruining her in the broadcasting business as she had feared, had sparked considerable interest among the powers-that-be. By the time she'd placed the last call, she had agreed to six interviews, five of which would take place in Seattle for her convenience.

The sixth, in San Francisco, was scheduled for her day off.

Still in something of a daze, Vanessa took a TV dinner from the freezer and shoved it into the microwave. She was eating breaded fish when the telephone rang.

"Job offers?" Nick asked, without extending a greeting or even identifying himself.

Vanessa sighed. "Interviews," she corrected. "Did you find a new chef?"

"No," he snapped, and his tone stung like a hard flick from a rubber band. "Did you find a new cleaning lady? Damn it, Vanessa, for once let's not evade the issue here. I'm in love with you, and you're about to be offered a job that takes you to another part of the country. It's half-time, and I'd like to know whether my team is winning or losing."

Vanessa's front teeth scraped her lower lip. "One of us could commute," she said, knowing the idea wasn't going to please him.

She could see Nick shove his hand through his hair so clearly that she might as well have been standing in the same room with him. "No way," he ground out.

Vanessa stood up very straight, bracing herself. Nick had been so gentle with her, so understanding, but now he was showing his true colors. Now he was going to be the demanding male, trying to dictate her life-style and the course her career would take.

He really was as arrogant and egotistical as Parker, he was just more subtle about it.

"I guess we don't have anything more to talk about," Vanessa said, and it took all her strength not to fall apart right then and there.

"We have everything to talk about," Nick argued. He sounded calmer, but there was a note of despair in his voice that told Vanessa they weren't going to be able to work out a compromise this time.

"Goodbye," she said brokenly, and then she hung up and covered her face with both hands.

For two weeks, Vanessa didn't see or talk to Nick. She met with the people sent to recruit her for their local newscasts and talk shows and spent the rest of her time selling merchandise over the Midas Network and telling herself that some people just weren't meant to have it all.

Of the offers she received, the one in San Francisco was the most promising—she would cohost a magazine-style program that had already been optioned for syndication over cable television. Her salary would be twice what she was earning at the Midas Network, and she had always had a special affection for the city by the bay.

Vanessa had chosen not to make any hard and fast decisions until she'd gotten her emotions on a more even keel, and she felt like a tightrope walker with no balance pole.

The day before Thanksgiving, Vanessa's grandmother called. "Are you absolutely positive you can't come over for dinner?" she asked plaintively. "It's been so long since your grampa and I have seen you, and you've been looking a little peaky lately. Either that or you shouldn't wear peach."

Vanessa smiled, despite the feeling of quiet despondency that had possessed her since the day she left Portland. "You've been watching the shopping channel again," she said, evading the question her grandmother had asked her about Thanksgiving.

Alice Bradshaw chuckled, but the sound was a little hollow. "I watch every day, sweetie. Last week, I even ordered a cordless screwdriver for your grandfather. Now, are you going to change your mind and come home or not?"

"I have to work," Vanessa apologized, pushing her hair back from her forehead and letting out a long breath. Actually that statement was slightly wide of the truth because she had had the day off but offered to fill in so that another host could spend the holiday with family. Even so, she wasn't in the mood to celebrate anything since Nick was out of her life.

Her grandmother was clearly disappointed. "Can we look for you to visit at Christmas, then?" she pressed.

Vanessa swallowed. Christmas seemed far away, though she knew it wasn't. Maybe by then she'd have a grip on herself. "Okay," she agreed, looking distractedly at the wall calendar on the pantry door. "It's a date."

Alice was clearly pleased and excited. "You could bring that young man of yours along—the one Rodney's been telling us about."

Vanessa closed her eyes, feeling as though she'd just been struck a blow to the midsection. *When I get through with you, Rodney Bradshaw,* she thought venomously, *it will take every chiropractic instructor in that school to put you back together.* "Nick and I aren't seeing each other anymore," she said with cheery bleakness. "How's Grampa?"

"What do you mean you aren't seeing Nick anymore?" Alice demanded, not to be put off by questions about the hearty health of her husband. "Rodney said this was *it!*"

"Rodney doesn't know what he's talking about," Vanessa said tightly.

Alice sighed. "I knew something was wrong by the way you looked. That man went and did you dirty, didn't he?"

Saying yes would have satisfied Alice, but Vanessa couldn't bring herself to lie. Nick had been stubborn, unbending and chauvinistic, but he hadn't made a deliberate effort to break her heart. "Nothing so dramatic," she confessed. "There were a few fundamental things we couldn't agree on, that's all."

The conversation ended a few minutes after that and, just as Vanessa was hanging up, Rodney rapped at the back door and let himself in.

He was obviously ready to make the long drive to Spokane. "Sure you don't want to go along?" he asked slyly.

Vanessa glared at him, her hands on her hips. "I wouldn't go anywhere with you, you big mouth," she said. "What did you mean by telling Gramma and Grampa about Nick?"

Rodney sighed. "Every time I called them they asked how you were getting along and whether or not you had a man in your life. I suppose I should have lied?"

"Of course not," Vanessa said, sagging a little.

"Call Nick," Rodney told her. "You're never going to be happy until you do."

Vanessa shook her head. Being a man, Rodney probably wouldn't understand if she explained, so she didn't make the effort.

One of Rodney's shoulders moved in a shrug. "It's your choice, of course. I'll see you on Monday, Van."

She accepted his brotherly kiss on the forehead. "Be careful," she couldn't stop herself from saying. "It's snowing on Snoqualmie Pass."

Rodney grinned. "I'll be okay," he promised, and then, after giving Vanessa a quick hug, he left.

It was time to leave for the studio, so she wrapped herself up in her warmest cloth coat, pulled a fuzzy green stocking cap onto her head and left the house.

When she arrived at work, a message awaited her. Paul wanted to see her in his office immediately.

Vanessa pulled off her stocking cap and coat as she walked down the hallway and knocked at her boss's door. While she hadn't actually given notice, it was common knowledge at the network that she wouldn't be renewing her contract.

Paul was standing when she stepped through his doorway. "Before we get down to business," he said when Vanessa was seated in a chair facing his desk, "I'm under strict orders to invite you to our house for dinner tomorrow night. We're having turkey and pumpkin pie—the whole bit. Say you'll be there and Janet will be off my back."

Vanessa smiled sadly and shook her head. "I'm in no mood to 'accidentally' run into your best friend," she said.

Paul sighed and spread his hands. "I tried. Janet had some idea that if your eyes met Nick's over the stuffing and candied yams, lightning would strike."

"Nick is going to be there, then?" Vanessa asked, unable to stop herself.

Paul shrugged. "I was going to ask him after you went to do your segment. Which brings me to the real reason I called you in here. The network is prepared to offer you a sizeable raise to stay on."

Vanessa lowered her eyes and shook her head, but after a few moments she met Paul's gaze steadily. "I hope you don't think I'm ungrateful," she said. "You gave me my first real job, and I'll never forget that."

There was a short silence, then Paul asked, "Have you made any decisions about where you'll go next?"

She sighed, thinking of her ordeal on that talk show with Parker and of the lurid stories that had come out in the tabloids a week afterward. BASEBALL GREAT RESCUES DRUNKEN EX, one of the headlines had read. It still amazed her that the publicity had helped her career instead of ending it once and for all. "No," she answered at last, "but I am leaning toward the job in San Francisco." It was the first time she'd admitted that, even to herself. She wanted to be a long way from the memories of Nick.

"You never heard from *Seattle This Morning*?"

Vanessa tried to smile as she shook her head. "Ironic, isn't it? They were probably the only ones who were put off by the article in the *National Snoop*."

"Nobody takes that rag seriously," Paul said, dismissing the subject. "We'll all be very sorry to see you go, Vanessa," he finished.

Vanessa couldn't answer since she had a lump in her throat the size of a football helmet. She paused in the doorway, though, and when she was able to speak again, she asked, "What was Nick's number? When he was still playing ball, I mean?"

Paul thought for a moment. "Fifty-eight, I think. Why?"

Vanessa shrugged. "I don't know," she answered, and when she looked back at Paul over one shoulder, there were tears glistening in her eyes.

Her boss got out of his chair, crossed the room and simultaneously closed the door and drew her into his arms. "Van, no job is worth this," he said.

"You wouldn't say that if I were a man," Vanessa wailed, completely miserable.

Paul chuckled. "I wouldn't be holding you if you were a man, either," he pointed out.

Vanessa began to sob as the enormity of losing Nick washed over her once again. It was like parting with a lung.

Paul led her back to the chair she'd just left, seated her and buzzed his secretary to ask her to bring in a glass of cold water.

"Nick is a reasonable man," he insisted once the secretary had gone. "I'm sure you could come to some kind of agreement if you'd just talk things over!"

She dabbed her eyes with a tissue plucked from the box on Paul's desk and then wadded it into a ball. She was a wreck; she had to pull herself together and stop moping around all the time. "When I was married to Parker," she said in the thick lisp of the terminally weepy, "I had to hand over all my dreams like a dowry. He didn't want me to go to college, so I quit. He didn't want children, so I gave up on the idea of having babies. Do you really wonder why I don't want to wake up one morning and find myself in the same trap with Nick?"

Paul sighed. "Take the rest of the day off, Vanessa—you're in no shape to sell ceiling fans. Mel is on a roll today—I'm sure he won't mind filling in for you."

Vanessa refused. She wouldn't have it said that she couldn't pull her own weight.

Fifteen minutes later she went on camera and started pitching musical jewelry boxes. Despite Margie's skill with makeup, a glance at the monitor assured Vanessa that she looked bad enough to scare Boris Karloff.

She was demonstrating the ugliest floor lamp in captivity when Oliver smilingly announced that it was time to take a call from a viewer.

"What's your name?" Vanessa's cohost asked, reaching out to touch the lamp fondly.

"Nick DeAngelo," responded the caller. "What's yours?"

Vanessa stepped on the base of the lamp at that moment, causing it to wave madly from side to side. She flung both arms around the thing just as it would have toppled to the floor.

"We've got to talk," Nick said. "Will you have dinner with me tonight, Vanessa?"

"No," Vanessa answered, and it was a struggle to get the word out.

"You're being stubborn," Nick insisted.

"Do you want a floor lamp or not?" Vanessa yelled, wondering when those jerks in the control booth were going to disconnect the call. It was obvious that this was no ordinary viewer.

Nick laughed. "I've missed you, too, babe," he said, and his voice was a brandy-and-cream rumble that brought pink color pulsing to Vanessa's cheeks.

The floor director seemed delighted. He stood beside one of the cameramen, signaling Vanessa to continue. Her chest swelled as she drew a deep, deliberate breath in an effort to keep her composure. She tried to smile, but the effort was hopeless.

"This is really not the time or place for this," she said, speaking as pleasantly as she could. "Some of our other viewers are probably anxious to talk to us about these lamps."

Again the item in question teetered dangerously; again Vanessa caught it just in time.

"Far be it from me to stand in the way of free enterprise," Nick replied. "I'll pick you up at seven-thirty."

Vanessa squared her shoulders and looked directly into the camera. "I've moved," she lied, hoping he would take the hint.

"I'll find you," Nick replied.

It was all she could do not to stomp her feet and scream in frustration. "All right, all right. If I agree to see you, will you hang up?"

"Absolutely," was the generous response.

"Then I'll see you at seven-thirty," Vanessa said moderately, seething inside.

The cameramen cheered and, at the end of her segment, Vanessa learned that the switchboard had been lighted up for the entire three hours she was on. It did seem that everybody loved a lover.

Vanessa stepped through her front door at five-fifteen, screamed in a belated release of her temper and hurled her purse across the living room. Her cat gave a terrified meow and fled up the stairs, and Vanessa was instantly contrite.

"I'm sorry," she called out, but it was no use. Sari would not forgive such a transgression unless Vanessa groveled and made an offering of creamed tuna.

Nick arrived promptly at seven-thirty, wearing the tuxedo he'd had on the first time Vanessa met him. He was as handsome as ever, although there was a hollow expression in his eyes.

He took in Vanessa's glimmery blue dress with appreciation as she stepped back to admit him. "I half expected that you would have moved out of state before I got here," he said.

Vanessa averted her eyes. She'd fantasized about seeing Nick again for days but, despite all those mental rehearsals, the reality was nearly overwhelming. She couldn't help hoping that he was ready to give some ground where their relationship was concerned so that they could forge some kind of future together.

"You look very dapper," she commented, ignoring his remark. The lapels of his coat were of glistening black satin, and it was difficult not to touch him.

"Thank you," he replied with a slight inclination of his head.

Vanessa, who earned her living by thinking on her feet, talking for as long as three hours virtually nonstop, was tongue-tied. All the things she longed to say to Nick were caught in her throat, practically choking her.

He seemed to be looking into her soul and reading her most private emotions. "It's all right," he said, touching her face briefly with one hand. "We'll find our way through all this somehow. I promise."

Vanessa wished she could be so sure. As he laid her velvet evening coat over her shoulders, she fought to hold back tears of confusion and fear.

A lot of people would have said she was crazy, she thought, as she and Nick whisked through the rainy night in his Corvette. Jock or no jock, this was a rare and gentle man, the kind most women would have tackled and hog-tied. And Paul had been right when he'd said that no job was worth the kind of pain the loss of Nick DeAngelo had caused her. As if that weren't enough, Vanessa knew she loved the man to distraction.

She'd been holding him at arm's length since the night they met, comparing him to Parker. Down deep, she'd known all along that Nick was as different from her ex-husband as salt was from sugar.

There could be only one reason for her failure to make a commitment, and that was fear—fear of loving and then losing, trusting and being betrayed.

The end of her relationship with Parker had been bitterly painful, even though she'd wanted the divorce and known that she had no other choice. If that happened with Nick, she knew she wouldn't be able to endure it.

She closed her eyes and let her head rest against the back of the seat.

"Don't be afraid, Vanessa," Nick said softly. "Please."

Vanessa looked at him, drew in the scent of his cologne. "That's like asking a burn victim not to be be scared of fire," she replied in a sad voice.

Nick sighed. "I'm not the guy who burned you," he reminded her. "Doesn't that mean anything?"

"You have more power over me than Parker ever dreamed of having," Vanessa admitted, unable to keep the words back. "If you wanted to, you could crush me so badly that I'd never find all the pieces."

He turned his head and glowered at her. "You're stronger than you think you are," he said, clearly annoyed. "Give yourself—and me—a little credit."

An uncomfortable silence settled over the car after that, and neither Nick nor Vanessa spoke until they'd reached DeAngelo's and been seated inside a private dining room.

Vanessa had never seen a more elegant room. There was a single table in front of a view of Elliot Bay. The streets were lighted up like a tangle of Christmas tree lights, the colors smudged by the rain that sheeted the windows. Candles provided the only light, and a violinist serenaded Nick and Vanessa as they sat looking at each other, comfortable with the music.

When the music stopped the first waiter appeared, bringing champagne. He popped the cork and poured the frothy liquid into their glasses, being very careful not to look at either Vanessa or Nick.

Vanessa arched an eyebrow the moment they were alone. "No diet cola?" she joked.

Nick grinned. "I'm trying to get past your defenses here, in case you haven't noticed."

"I've noticed," Vanessa said with a sigh, clinking her glass against Nick's as he lifted it in a toast.

"To page 72," he said.

Vanessa laughed and sipped her wine. For the first time in days she felt whole and human. It would be so easy to give herself to Nick body and soul, and that was exactly why she had to keep herself under control.

"I saw a shadow in your eyes just now," Nick said, reaching across the table to take her hand in his. "What were you thinking about?"

"Guess."

His jawline tightened then relaxed again. "The perils of loving Nick DeAngelo?" he ventured.

Vanessa nodded and looked away toward the harbor. "Did Paul and Janet invite you over for Thanksgiving dinner?" she asked in an attempt to change the subject. God knew, the one at hand was a blind alley.

His hand gripped hers for a moment, then moved away. "Yes," he said. "Vanessa, look at me."

She hated the fact that her first impulse was always to do exactly what Nick told her. Before she could do anything about it, her gaze had shifted to his face. "Don't make this any more difficult than it already is," she pleaded. "Please."

"Will you come home with me tonight?"

Vanessa wanted to be flippant. "You move fast," she said, and immediately felt like a bumbling teenager.

"Vanessa."

"No," she said quickly. "No, I won't sleep with you, Nick."

"Why not?"

The nerve. "Because pilgrims don't sleep around, that's why."

Nick tilted his head to one side and studied her. "What?" he asked, looking honestly puzzled.

She smiled, albeit very sadly. "Tomorrow morning I have to get up, put on a pilgrim costume and sell my little heart out. Does that answer your question?"

"Not by a long shot," Nick grumbled as a second waiter appeared with enormous salads.

Vanessa ate with good appetite, having learned her lesson about too much wine on an empty stomach, and by the time the broiled lobster had been served, she felt almost human.

Dessert made her positively daring. When Nick took her home, she invited him in for a drink.

The living room was dark, but Vanessa didn't bother to turn on a light since there was virtually no furniture to bump into. She was leading the way toward the kitchen when a crash and groan behind her made her leap for the switch.

Nick was sprawled on the floor on his back, looking for all the world like someone who had fallen off a ten-story building.

Vanessa dropped to her knees beside him. "Are you all right?" she cried.

"My back is out," he answered, moaning.

There was no time to be wasted. Vanessa went right to the heart of the matter and panicked. She scrambled for the afghan her grandmother had knitted and covered him with it as if he were a war casualty. His eyes were closed, and he was pale.

"Nick, say something!" she cried.

"I may sue," he replied.

10

Vanessa tapped one foot nervously while she waited for Gina to answer the telephone. Finally she heard a breathless "hello" at the other end of the line.

Huddled in her kitchen, speaking in a whisper, Vanessa explained that Nick was lying in the middle of her living room floor, apparently immobilized. "What should I do?" she asked. "Call the paramedics?"

Gina laughed. "It would serve him right if you did. Nick's faking, Vanessa—he probably wants to spend the night."

Vanessa sighed. Of course Nick was pretending, indulging his hypochondria. After all this was the man who carried on like a victim of Lizzie Borden's when he cut himself. "Thank you," she said.

"See you tomorrow," Gina responded lightly. "Have fun getting Nick off the floor."

"Tomorrow?"

"At Uncle Guido's dinner, of course," came the answer.

Vanessa's hackles rose. Evidently Nick had committed her to a family gathering without so much as consulting her. She said a polite goodbye to Gina and, after gathering her dignity, walked back into the living room.

There, standing beside Nick's prone body, she folded her arms across her chest and nudged him with one foot. "What's happening at your Uncle Guido's place tomorrow, Nick?"

With great and obvious anguish, Nick raised himself to a sitting position. "I could have been killed," he fretted, avoiding her question.

"That could still happen," Vanessa allowed.

Laboriously the man who had once struck fear into the heart of every linebacker in the National Football League hauled himself to his feet. He gave the vacuum cleaner he'd tripped over a look that should have melted the plastic handle, and then sighed. "I suppose you're mad because I told my family you'd come to dinner tomorrow afternoon," he said.

Vanessa was tapping one foot again. "That kind of high-handed presumption is exactly what keeps me from marrying you, Nick DeAngelo!"

He leaned close to her, and she was filled with the singular scent of him. His dark eyes were snapping with annoyance. "Who asked you to get married, Lawrence?" he countered.

Crimson heat filled Vanessa's face. No one, not even Parker, could make her as furious, so fast, as Nick could. "You wanted to shack up?" she seethed.

Nick sighed again heavily. "Time out," he said, making the signal with his hands. "Let's start over. You're the one who brought up the subject of marriage."

Vanessa looked away, her eyes filling with sudden embarrassing tears. She had no idea what to say.

Nick took her arms into his hands and made her look at him. "It's time we stopped playing games," he said hoarsely. "I love you, Vanessa, and I'd like nothing better than to marry you. Tonight, tomorrow, whenever you say."

Vanessa bit into her lower lip. She wanted to say yes so badly that she could barely hold the word back, but fear stopped her. Mortal fear that gripped her mind and spirit like an iron fist, cold and inescapable. She tried to get past it, like a mountain climber working her way around an obstacle by inching along a narrow ledge.

"Maybe I wasn't so far off a minute ago," she ventured to say, "when I asked if you wanted to live together."

Nick stared at her in wounded amazement. "You said 'shack up,' if I remember correctly," he replied.

Vanessa winced at the dry fury in his tone and rushed headlong into her subject. "It seems to me that it would be a good idea for us to live together for a while, just until we could make sure we really love each other."

Nick's eyes glowed with dark heat. "Sure," he mocked, shrugging. "That way you wouldn't have to make a commitment. If you got a job offer in another city, or decided you wanted a different roommate, you could just bail out!"

"That isn't what I meant at all!" Vanessa cried, horrified at the picture he was painting.

"Isn't it?" he demanded. "Tell me, Vanessa— where were we going to set up this romantic little love nest?"

She swallowed. "I thought San Francisco would be nice," she admitted in a very small voice.

"I'll bet you did," Nick retorted, and, unbelievably, he turned and strode toward the door.

Vanessa hurried after him, not wanting to let him go again so soon. "Nick, wait . . ."

He stopped and turned to face her, but there was a cold distance in his eyes that made her heart ache. "I want a wife and a family, Vanessa—I've told you that. If you can't make a commitment, then for God's sake let me go."

"You're being a prude," Vanessa accused, as he opened the door to an icy November wind.

"Imagine," Nick marveled, spreading his hands. "Me—the party animal. Go figure it."

"Don't be so stubborn and unreasonable!" Vanessa cried, knowing how lonely her world was without him. "Lots of people are living together these days, and they're making their relationships work!"

"Good for them," Nick replied. "As for me, I'm ready for a wife, not a perennial girlfriend. Sleep tight, Vanessa." With that, he went out, closing the door crisply behind him.

Feeling bereft, Vanessa shot the bolt into place and wandered witlessly back to the kitchen, meaning to console herself with a cup of tea. She'd turned her answering machine off to call Gina earlier, and now, after putting a mug of water into the microwave, she checked for messages.

There was only one, but it might have made all the difference in the world if she'd only heard it a few minutes earlier. The producers of *Seattle This Morning* wanted her to host the show, not with a partner, but on her own.

Vanessa would have jumped for joy at any other time, but she couldn't forget that Nick had just walked out the front door. She dreaded facing the rest of her life without him.

Thursday was long and it was lonely. Vanessa did her stint on the shopping channel—dressed as a pilgrim—and turned down numerous invitations to friends' houses opting instead to go home alone and cook a frozen turkey dinner in her microwave.

There were messages on her machine from everyone in the world except Nick DeAngelo. She returned a happy-holiday call to her grandparents and left the others unanswered. All night she lay staring up at the ceiling, trying to imagine herself living with Nick as his wife, bearing his children, sharing his joys and his problems.

The pleasant pictures were all too fleeting. It was easier to imagine him packing to leave her on some rainy afternoon.

All night Vanessa tossed and turned. Long before morning she knew what she had to do. If she stayed in Seattle, she would keep having destructive encounters with Nick, which would break her heart over and over again.

She had to start over somewhere else.

She called the television station in San Francisco first and told them she was accepting their offer, and then she got in touch with a friend in real estate and arranged to put her house on the market. She hoped the new owners would let Rodney go on living in the garage apartment since he liked it so much.

Nick didn't try to contact her again, and Vanessa's feelings about that were mixed. She marveled at her own capacity for conflicting emotions where that man was concerned.

When the fifteenth of December finally arrived, Vanessa's brief career with the Midas Network was over. That evening Mel and the Harmons shanghaied her, dragging her off to a farewell party at, of all places, DeAngelo's.

"How could you?" Vanessa demanded of Janet Harmon in a whisper when the crowd of people from the network had finished congratulating her and gone back to enjoying wine and hors d'oeuvres. It would have been easier if Nick had been away looking after the other restaurant or something, but he was very much in evidence.

"How could I?" Janet echoed. "Vanessa, how could *you*? Leaving the Midas Network is one thing, but leaving Nick is another. Are you out of your mind? The man adores you!"

Vanessa's gaze went involuntarily to Nick. He was talking to a couple on the far side of the restaurant, laughing at something the woman said as he drew back her chair. Knowing all the while that her reaction was silly, Vanessa ached with jealousy. "Bringing me here was a rotten trick," she said miserably, forcing her eyes back to her own circle. "Thanks a lot."

"We were trying to bring you to your senses, that's all," argued Mel, leaning forward in his chair. He was accompanied by a woman half his age with bleached hair and whisk-broom eyelashes.

Vanessa sighed. "Even if I wanted to stay, it's too late. I've already given up my job and sold my house."

Paul, now her former boss, sat back in his chair. "The spot on *Seattle This Morning* is still open," he said.

Vanessa felt a little leap of hope in a corner of her heart, but it died quickly. She was as afraid of commitment as she'd ever been, and Nick probably didn't want her anymore anyway.

She wasn't about to find out. Going to him with heart in her hands and being rejected would be more than she could bear. She looked down at the glass of chablis a waiter had poured for her moments before and left Paul's remark hanging unanswered in the air.

Vanessa was in a sort of daze from then on, eating her dinner, sipping her wine, making the proper responses—she hoped—to the things the other people around the large table said to her. She told herself that she had only to get through dessert and a round of goodbyes and then she could escape.

She was coming back from the rest room when she encountered Nick in the hallway. He blocked her way like Italy's answer to Goliath.

"Hello, Nick," she managed to choke out, her cheeks coloring. "How are you?"

He gave her a look that said her question was too stupid to rate an answer and sighed. "It would be easier to forget you if you weren't so damned beautiful," he said raggedly.

Vanessa didn't know what to say in response to that. Inwardly she cursed Janet for having her going-away party here where she couldn't have escaped seeing Nick. She tried to step around him but he wouldn't let her pass.

"It's damn easy for you to walk away, isn't it?" he asked in a low, wondering voice. "Didn't any of what happened between us get past that wall of ice you hide behind and touch you?"

Anguish filled Vanessa, but she refused to let her feelings show. She met Nick's gaze, a feat that nearly brought her to her knees. "It was all a game," she lied coldly.

Nick grasped her shoulders in his powerful hands. "If it was," he bit off the words, "we both lost."

Vanessa was on the verge of tears, but she kept her composure and stepped out of his hold. "Goodbye, Nick," she said in a soft voice. This time, when she went to walk away, he allowed her to pass.

She didn't stop at the table and speak to her friends; that was beyond her. She simply kept walking, crossing the dining room, concentrating on holding herself together.

She paused to collect her coat, but she was practically running when she reached the sidewalk.

Snow was drifting down from the sky in great lacy puffs—an unusual event in Seattle—and the magic eased Vanessa's tormented spirit just a little. She slowed her pace, allowing the weather to remind her of Spokane, of childhood and innocence.

Pike Place Market, with its noise and bustle, reminded her that she was in Seattle. She went inside, making her way through hordes of happy Christmas shoppers, pausing in front of a fish market, watching and listening as salmon and cod and red snapper were weighed and tossed on the counter to be wrapped. Vanessa stepped closer.

"Help you, lady?" asked a young boy with dark hair and eyes. He was wearing a white apron over jeans and a sweatshirt, and Vanessa wondered if he was a part of Nick's vast family.

Vanessa stepped closer, feeling self-conscious in her glittering blue dress, strappy shoes and evening coat. She opened her evening bag to make sure that she had money. "I-I'll take a pound of— of red snapper, please."

"Red snapper, a pound!" the boy yelled toward the back of the market, and the weighing and tossing process started all over again.

"What's your name?" Vanessa asked.

The young man gave her an odd look. "Mark," he said. "Mark DeAngelo."

She smiled. Nick had told her about working in his uncle's fish market when he was about Mark's age. For Vanessa, it was like looking into the past, seeing Nick as he must have been. "You're Gina's cousin?"

Mark nodded, taking Vanessa's money and making change, still looking puzzled.

Vanessa felt foolish. She put her change back into her purse and reached out for the red snapper, now snug in its white package.

"You a friend of Gina's?" Mark asked just as Vanessa would have turned and walked away.

"Nick's," she confessed.

His wonderful dark eyes narrowed. "So you're the one," he said, and any friendliness he might have shown earlier had faded away.

Vanessa swallowed, wondering what had brought her to this market in the dark of night, what had made her mention Nick in the first place.

"Uncle Guido," the boy said to a heavyset man who had materialized beside him. "This is her— Nick's lady."

Guido DeAngelo gave his nephew a quelling look, then smiled at Vanessa and extended one hand over the counter where crab legs and salmon steaks lay on a bed of ice. "You forgive Mark," he pleaded, beaming. "He got no manners. No good manners at all."

Vanessa shifted her bag and her package of fish so that she could shake Guido's hand. "How do you do?" she murmured, completely at a loss for anything more imaginative to say.

Guido's bright dark eyes took in her evening clothes and her special hairstyle. "You have new fight with Nicky?" he demanded. Despite his stern manner, Vanessa doubted that he had a trace of malice in him.

The tears came back. "I'm afraid it's an old fight," she answered.

Guido rounded the counter and hugged her. "That Nicky. He's a stubborn one. You tell him his Uncle Guido said to quit it out right now!"

"Quit it out?" Vanessa echoed.

"Cut it out," Mark translated from his position at the cash register.

Vanessa smiled and nodded. "I'll tell him," she promised. *If I ever see him again.*

Outside the market, Vanessa hailed a cab. She half hoped to find Nick's Corvette waiting in her driveway, but the only car in evidence was her own. She paid the driver and hurried around to the back door.

The telephone was ringing when she stepped inside the house, and she heard the answering machine pick up and play its recorded spiel.

"Damn it," Janet Harmon said, "I know you're there, Vanessa Lawrence. Pick up the phone right now or I swear I'll come over and bring the whole party with me!"

Vanessa literally dove for the receiver. "Don't," she cried, "please! I'm here!"

"Well," Janet retorted, "if it isn't the disappearing guest of honor. You might have told us you were leaving, you know."

Vanessa lowered her head, feeling guilty. Her friends had gone to a great deal of work and expense to say farewell, and she had left them high and dry. "I'm sorry," she said. "It's just that—"

"Don't tell me," Janet interrupted, "I can guess. You ran into Nick, went a few rounds with him for old times' sake and then crawled off to lick your wounds."

Vanessa was incensed. "It wasn't like that at all," she said, even as one part of her insisted that Janet was exactly right. Mostly in self-defense, she began to get angry. "In some ways, Janet, it serves you right. If you'd picked any other restaurant besides DeAngelo's, this wouldn't have happened!"

Janet was quiet for a moment while Vanessa regretted having spoken so sharply.

"I'm sorry," they both said in unison. After that they laughed in chorus, and then cried.

"What are your plans for the holidays?" Janet wanted to know when they'd each gotten a hold on themselves.

"I'm going home to visit my grandparents," Vanessa said.

"After that?"

"I'm due in San Francisco on January second."

"Do you have an apartment?"

Vanessa glanced at the clock, stretching the telephone cord so that she could walk to the refrigerator and toss the package of red snapper inside. "No," she answered. "The station is putting me up in a hotel until I can find something. Where are you calling from?"

"Nick's office," Janet replied. "The party's still in full swing—why don't you come back?"

Vanessa relived the encounter she'd had with Nick in the hallway and nearly doubled over from the pain the memory caused her. "I couldn't," she said.

"What did you say to each other?" Janet wanted to know. "You sound like someone in Intensive Care, and I think Nick is out on a ledge even as we speak."

"What do we always say to each other?" Vanessa countered. She knew the question would confuse Janet, and that was exactly what she wanted. "Listen, my friend—Nick DeAngelo is old news, all right? I don't want to talk about him anymore. Not tonight, at least."

Janet sighed heavily. "Okay," she conceded. "But let me go on record as one who thinks some of your wires are stripped."

Vanessa smiled sadly, though there was no one there to see her. "Thank you for giving the party—I really appreciate it, even though I didn't behave as if I did."

"I understand," Janet said. And that was why she was such a good friend—Vanessa knew without a doubt that she really did. "Will we see you again before Christmas?"

Vanessa promised not to leave Seattle without saying goodbye and hung up. She didn't sleep well that night, but that was nothing new.

In the morning she was up early. Dressed in jeans, sneakers and a flannel shirt, she was busy packing in the living room when Rodney startled her out of her skin by bursting into the room from the kitchen.

He was dragging an enormous Christmas tree behind him.

"You didn't," Vanessa said painfully, looking at the evidence. The lush scent filled the near-empty room.

Rodney beamed. "Yes, Lady Scrooge, I did. You're going to have a tree whether you like it or not!"

"I'm not even going to be here!" Vanessa wailed.

"Where's your Christmas spirit?" Rodney demanded, looking hurt.

Vanessa had never been able to take a hard line with Rodney. Loving him was a lifetime habit. She shoved a hand through her hair. "Do you promise to take it down before we go home? The Wilsons want to move in the first week in January."

Rodney was mollified. "You have my word, Van. I'll not only take it down, but I'll vacuum up the pine needles and the stray tinsel."

Vanessa laughed. "Wild promises, those," she said just as the doorbell rang.

A delivery man was standing on the porch holding a massive pink poinsettia in a pot wrapped in gold foil and tied with a wide white ribbon. Vanessa accepted the plant, scrounged up a tip and tore open the card the moment she'd closed the door.

"Let's part friends," it read. "Call me. Nick."

A hard, aching lump formed in Vanessa's throat, and tears smarted in her eyes. Against her better judgment and without a word to Rodney, she stepped into the kitchen and dialed the familiar number.

Nick's secretary answered on the second ring.

Vanessa introduced herself and was put through to him directly.

"Thanks for the poinsettia," she said.

"I'm sorry about last night," Nick replied.

Vanessa hugged herself with one arm. Just the sound of his voice tied her in knots; she wondered what she was going to do without him. "Me, too," she answered.

"You've sold your house," he said, evidently determined to keep the ball rolling.

"I should have done it a long time ago." Vanessa wondered what kind of talk show host she was going to make when she could hardly carry on an intelligent conversation with the man she loved more than life.

"I guess you'll want a small place when you get to San Francisco," he ventured.

So he knew she'd accepted the job there. Vanessa closed her eyes for a moment. "Probably," she responded.

"I'd like to see you before you leave."

Nick's words shouldn't have surprised Vanessa, but they did. It was a long time before she could speak.

"I wonder if that's such a good idea." Her voice was faint and shaky. "We don't seem to do very well on a one-to-one basis."

Nick gave a hollow chuckle. "There's an obvious response to that remark, but I'll let it pass out of chivalry."

Vanessa had to smile. "Is that what you call it?" she countered.

"I hear you met my uncle last night."

She let out her breath. "Yes."

"He gave me a long, loud lecture about mistreating lovely ladies," Nick went on.

Vanessa laughed softly. "I suppose I looked pretty forlorn," she confessed.

"I'm sorry," he responded, his voice a velvety caress.

"Did Uncle Guido tell you to say that?" Vanessa teased.

"Yes," Nick answered. "As a matter of fact, that was part of my penance. Vanessa, will you spend the afternoon with me?"

"I've got to pack and do some Christmas shopping—"

"Please?" he persisted. And when Nick persisted, he was nearly irresistible.

"There's no point—"

"I'm not going to pressure you, Van," Nick broke in gently. "All I'm asking for is this afternoon, not the rest of your life."

It took Vanessa a long time to answer. She wished she had the courage to offer the rest of her life, but she didn't. "Okay," she said.

Nick came to get her at noon, dressed casually in jeans, a turtleneck sweater and a leather jacket. There was a sad glow in his coffee-colored eyes as he took in Vanessa's gray slacks and sweater.

"Hi," he said.

Vanessa resisted an urge to hurl herself into his arms and beg him never to hurt her, never to betray or reject her. "Hi," she answered.

They went to Pike Place Market and walked through it, hand in hand, visiting the different shops and talking about everything but Vanessa's new job and her impending move to California. They had lunch in a fish bar on the waterfront and then drove to a Christmas-tree lot well outside the heart of the city.

Nick inspected tree after tree, consulting Vanessa about each one. She played a dangerous game in her heart, pretending that they would always be together at Christmas, selecting trees, stuffing stockings, putting dolls and tricycles out for little ones to find.

"How are you going to get that home?" Vanessa wanted to know when Nick had at last settled on a seven-foot noble pine with a luscious scent.

Nick looked puzzled by her question. With the help of the attendant, he bound the enormous tree to the top of his Corvette, and Vanessa held her breath the whole time.

She couldn't help comparing Nick's apparent carefree attitude with Parker's paranoia about his car's paint job.

The tree rode with them in the elevator, scratching their faces and shedding its perfume.

"I didn't get any shopping done," Vanessa complained, once they'd dragged the tree inside Nick's condominium and set it up in a waiting stand.

He was dusting his hands together. "I need to get something for Gina," he said. "Let's hit the mall."

Vanessa did a lot more pretending that afternoon, but, like all fantasies, her time with Nick had to end. When he saw her to her door, he didn't even try to kiss her.

"You really didn't pressure me," she marveled as he turned to walk away.

Nick looked back at her over one shoulder, his soul in his eyes. "When I make a promise," he said, "it's good forever."

Vanessa swallowed, thinking of promises that involved loving, honoring and cherishing. "W-will I see you again?" she asked.

He shrugged. "That's up to you," he said. "The next move is yours."

With that Nick walked away without looking back.

11

Their grandparents' Christmas tree was a muddle of color in the front window, and Rodney and Vanessa exchanged a look of delight as they pulled into the familiar driveway.

John and Alice Bradshaw had heard the distinctive purr of the sports car's motor and were huddled together on the front porch, waiting. Rodney and Vanessa raced up the walk to greet them with exuberant hugs.

"It's about time you got here," John complained good-naturedly, and then he and Rodney went off to carry in the presents and suitcases that were jammed in the little car.

Vanessa, in the meantime, was led into the kitchen by her spritely redheaded grandmother and divested of her coat and purse. The room was filled with the scents of Christmas—cinnamon, peppermint, a hint of evergreen from the boughs surrounding the striped candle at the center of the table.

"I'm so glad to be home," Vanessa said, and then, remarkably, she burst into tears.

Alice made a clucking sound with her tongue and squired her granddaughter to a seat at the table. "Tell me all about it, sweetheart," she said, patting Vanessa's hand.

Rodney and John had arrived with their arms full by then, and Alice had to go and open the door for them. Vanessa waited with her head down until her cousin and grandfather had passed diplomatically into the living room.

"It's Nick, isn't it?" Alice persisted once they were alone again. She'd brewed a pot of tea, and she poured cupfuls for herself and Vanessa before sitting down.

Vanessa had regained some control of herself. "He's so unbelievably wonderful," she sniffled, plucking a tissue from the little packet that was stuffed into a pocket of her sweater. She was getting to be a regular old maid, carrying on all the time and having to stave off bouts of weeping.

Alice arched one finely shaped eyebrow. At sixty-seven she was still a lovely woman. Her green eyes were as bright and full of humor and love as ever, and her skin was flawless. She wore her rich auburn hair in a braided chignon and dressed in cotton shirtwaist dresses. Vanessa adored her.

"That's what you said about Parker," the older woman remarked.

Vanessa sighed. "I know," she said. "That's part of the problem—what happened with Parker, I mean." She paused to pull in a deep, shaky breath and let it out again. "Nick used to be a professional football player."

Alice was apparently reserving judgment on that, for she took a sip of her tea and shrugged in a way that meant for Vanessa to continue.

"He was a party animal, too," Vanessa elaborated, thinking, for the first time, how thin her argument sounded. "Surrounded by women," she added uncertainly.

Alice didn't look convinced. "Lots of men carry on like that when they're younger," she observed. "Parker probably won't ever stop."

Vanessa sighed as memories flipped through her mind like rapidly turning pages in a scrapbook— Nick running backward in the park so that she could keep up, eating spaghetti at that café on the island, bringing the lightning inside while he loved her, tying a Christmas tree to the roof of his Corvette.

"I'm so scared, Gramma," Vanessa confessed, and her teacup rattled in its saucer as she set it down.

"But you love him?"

"More than my life," Vanessa answered.

"How about your fear? Is your love greater than that?"

Vanessa bit her lip. "No one in the world has more power to hurt me than Nick DeAngelo does," she said.

"There are two sides to that coin," Alice reminded her with a certain loving sternness in her voice. "No one else could make you happier, either—did you ever think of that? There are times in this life when we come to a crossroad, Vanessa, and we have to make a choice."

Vanessa looked down at her hands. "I've already made the choice," she said, even though she'd told her grandparents about her decision to move to San Francisco soon after it was made.

"Choices can be unmade. Vanessa, if Nick is a good man—and Rodney certainly seems to think he is—and you love him, then take the risk, for pity's sake!"

"What if he dies?" Vanessa whispered. "What if he decides he doesn't love me anymore and runs off with another woman?"

Alice looked exasperated. "What if you both live to be a hundred-and-four and die loving each other as much as you do today? You're being silly, Vanessa—silly and cowardly.

"Remember how it was when we'd go to the lake in the summertime when you were a little girl? You'd stand on the bank, dipping your toes in the water for an eternity while all your cousins were already swimming. By the time you finally took the plunge, the rest of us were ready to go home and you cried because you'd missed all the fun."

Vanessa smiled ruefully, recalling those incidents and others like them. She'd always been too cautious, except when she'd married Parker and that resounding failure had only made her more careful than ever before. "I am a bit of a coward, aren't I?"

"I don't want you thinking badly of yourself," Alice said firmly. "You're not the most daring person I've ever known, but there's something to be said for thinking things through and taking the slow and steady course, too."

"But I could be more of a risk taker," Vanessa ventured.

"Where this new man is concerned, I think you could," Alice allowed, pouring herself a second cup of tea.

That night, sleeping in her childhood bed in a room where cheerleading pom-poms and pictures of movie stars still graced the walls, Vanessa thought of the last time she'd seen Nick. *The next move is yours,* he'd said.

In the morning, Vanessa awakened and went downstairs in her old chenille bathrobe to find her grandfather in the living room, building the fire in the Franklin stove. John's blue eyes twinkled beneath bristly Santa Claus brows as he looked at her.

"Good morning, sunshine," he said. "You're up early."

A thick Spokane snowfall was wafting past the windows that overlooked the street. Vanessa went to her grandfather and kissed his cheek. "So are you," she pointed out. "But that's nothing new, is it?"

He closed the door of the stove, put the poker away and smiled at her. "We're going to miss tuning in the shopping channel and seeing you there every day," he said.

Vanessa glanced at the clock and wondered if Nick was still in bed or out running through wet, dark streets. Then she slipped her arm through her grandfather's and teased, "You were probably spending too much money trying to make me look good."

John laughed. "You don't need any help to look good, button—you never did." He paused, watching her with wise, gentle eyes. "And the way you keep looking at the clock makes me think maybe there's somebody you want to call."

Vanessa swallowed. She'd been thinking all night, and she'd decided her grandmother was right. It was time she gritted her teeth and took a chance. "There is," she confessed. "But I don't think I'm ready to do it yet."

The old man shrugged. "No one can decide when the time is right but you," he said, and he and Vanessa went into the kitchen where he poured fresh coffee for them both.

"Did you ever wish you hadn't married Gramma?" Vanessa asked, watching the snow through the window above the sink. It gave her a peaceful, secure feeling.

"A thousand and one times," John answered. "And I'm sure she wished she'd never laid eyes on me now and again, too."

Vanessa was staring at her grandfather in surprise, the lovely and mystical snow forgotten. "But you love each other!"

"That's no guarantee that two people are going to get along all the time, Vanessa," her grandfather pointed out reasonably, leaning against the counter as he sipped his coffee. "Show me a marriage where neither party ever gets mad and yells, and I'll show you a marriage where one or both partners just don't give a damn."

Vanessa made swift calculations. Christmas was just three days away. Perhaps, if she were very lucky, she could get a plane back to Seattle, do what she she needed to do and be home in time for the festivities.

She dived for the telephone book, flipped through until she found the number she needed and called a high-school friend who now worked as a travel agent.

Rose was delighted to hear from Vanessa and confessed to buying an exercise machine during one of her segments on the Midas Network. There was not, however, an available seat on any of the planes leaving Spokane until after Christmas.

Discouraged, Vanessa called the train station. The prospects were much more encouraging there, but when she hung up she saw her grandmother standing nearby, looking sad.

"I'll be back before Christmas, I promise," Vanessa said.

Alice was a woman who had made bravery a habit. She squared her shoulders. "Bring the football player back with you," she ordered, tightening the belt on her bathrobe and then smoothing her hair with one hand.

"I'll try," Vanessa promised. She took only her purse and coat, leaving her suitcase and gifts as a pledge that she would return.

The train trip was slow—it took eight hours—but the journey gave Vanessa plenty of time to assemble her thoughts. It was six o'clock in the evening when she reached downtown Seattle, and catching a cab turned to be such a competitive pursuit that it might have become an Olympic event.

Finally, however, she reached DeAngelo's and hurried upstairs to Nick's office, where he'd kissed her the night they met.

A middle-aged secretary looked her over warily. "Ms. Lawrence?" she echoed after Vanessa introduced herself. "You're Nicky's friend?"

Nicky. Vanessa bit back a smile and nodded. "Yes."

The secretary made a harrumph sound, as if to say "some friend," and then announced, "He's not here. Mr. DeAngelo is sick today."

Vanessa was alarmed. "Sick? What's the matter with him?"

A shrug was the only answer forthcoming, so Vanessa hastily excused herself and ran outside again. Cabs were still at a premium with so many last-minute shoppers in the downtown area, and it wasn't far to Nick's building. She hurried there on foot and was breathless when she fell against his doorbell.

"Who is it?" yelled a thick voice from inside.

Vanessa smiled. "It's Mrs. Santa Claus. Let me in!"

The door was wrenched open, and Nick stood in the chasm, wrapped in a blue terry-cloth robe. He smelled of mentholated rub, and his hair stood up in ridges as though he'd run greasy fingers through it.

Vanessa wrinkled her nose and stepped past him. "Your secretary tells me you're sick," she said.

Nick sneezed loudly. "I've seen colds like this develop into pneumonia," he said.

Vanessa rolled her eyes, but let the remark pass. After slipping out of her coat and laying it across a chair, she started toward the kitchen. "What you need is some hot lemon juice and honey," she said.

Nick stopped her by grasping her arm in one hand and whirling her around to face him. "What are you doing here?" he asked.

Inside she was trembling. She felt like a person standing on the edge of a cliff, about to pilot a hang glider for the first time. "You said the next move was mine. This is it, handsome."

His mouth dropped open. "You mean—"

"I mean that I love you, Nick."

"Wait a second. You've said that before. What's changed?"

"My mind. I'm not going to San Francisco, Nick, and if you still want to marry me . . ."

He gave a shout of joy, crushed her against him and whirled her around as though she weighed nothing at all. The scent of mentholated rub was nearly overpowering. "If? Baby, you just say when!"

Vanessa made a face as he set her back on her feet. "You smell awful," she said.

"God, this is romantic," Nick enthused, beaming. He sprinted off down the hall, and Vanessa set about finding lemon juice and honey.

When Nick returned minutes later, he'd showered and pulled on jeans and a T-shirt with the number 58 imprinted on the front. His hair was still damp and tousled, and Vanessa combed it with her fingers, smiling at his miraculous recovery.

He kissed her, and Vanessa knew she would catch his virus—if he had one—but she didn't care. When he lifted her into his arms, she made no protest.

"Just how long do you want me to stick around, woman?" he asked, his lips close to hers.

Vanessa touched his mouth with her own. "Only forever," she replied.

He kissed her again. "You've got it," he promised.

His bed was unmade and rumpled, but Vanessa barely noticed. She gave herself up to sweet anticipation as Nick removed her clothing article by article, making a game of kissing and caressing each part of her as he unveiled it.

Vanessa settled deep into the mattress of the water bed, giving a sigh of contentment, trusting Nick so fully that she clasped the headboard in her hands and abandoned herself completely to his loving.

He was tender, sensing that she was giving him her whole self this time and not just her body. She whimpered with pleasure as he circled one nipple with the tip of his tongue and held on tight to the headboard lest she drift away.

Nick teased her nipple, rolling it between his tongue and his teeth, then took it hungrily. When he'd had his fill of her breasts, he moved down over her quivering belly, taking tantalizing nips at her satin-smooth skin and deepening her whimper to a soft, steady croon.

And then he lifted her up in both hands, as he might take water from a cool, clean stream, and drank of her. The glory of it stunned her, but soon she was in a delirium of pleasure, tossing her head from side to side and letting go of the headboard to tangle her fingers in his hair. Shameless pleas fell from her lips, which felt dry even though she continuously ran her tongue over them, and her body was in mutiny against her mind, wildly seeking its own solace.

She sobbed his name as he brought her over the brink and introduced her to a new world—a world of unchained lightning and velvet fire. Her face was wet with tears when he finally poised himself above her, asking for her permission with his eyes.

Vanessa nodded, unable to speak, and ran her hands up and down the taut, corded muscles of Nick's back as he eased himself inside her. The pleasure was quiet at first—she'd already been wholly satisfied—but watching Nick's climb toward glory excited her all over again. When he reached the pinnacle, shuddering upon her and giving a fierce lunge of his hips, Vanessa met him there, arching her back to accommodate him, crying out in triumph and submission.

He buried his face in the curve of her neck when it was over, still trembling and breathing raggedly. Vanessa caressed him gently, wanting to soothe him.

Her body was utterly relaxed, but her mind was active. "I did promise my grandparents that I would come home for Christmas," she said. "They want me to bring you."

Nick sighed, his breath warm against her flesh. "Okay, but don't make any plans for next year without consulting me."

"Yes, sir!" Vanessa laughed.

He raised his head and gave her a sound, smacking kiss on the mouth. "Don't give me the old 'yes, sir' routine," he said, trying not to grin. "You're going to be nothing but trouble, woman, and you know it."

Vanessa was nibbling at his neck, giving him back some of his own. "Um-hmm," she agreed "trouble."

Nick groaned as she slid downward beneath him, tasting first one of his nipples and then the other. "Give me a break," he pleaded. "I'm Italian, not superhuman."

Vanessa giggled beneath Nick and the covers. "Same thing, to hear you tell it," she said. She didn't stop, and Nick was finally forced to submit to her attentions.

He was a very good loser.

The train pulled into Spokane at 11:50 p.m. on December 23rd, and Nick and Vanessa caught a cab to her grandparents' house.

Golden light spilled onto the snow outside their windows. "They're waiting up," Vanessa said, touched. "That's so sweet."

Nick paid the cabdriver and collected his suitcases, obviously nervous. "What if they don't like me?" he asked.

Vanessa smiled, pulling him toward the front door. "After the buildup Rodney's been giving you, they won't be able to help it," she said.

Her grandmother hurled open the door just as they reached it and hauled them inside. The Christmas tree glittered in front of the window, piled high with gifts, and a cheerful fire danced in the Franklin stove.

"So this is Nick?" Alice demanded looking him over.

"Number fifty-eight," John said reverently, extending a hand to his future grandson-in-law.

Vanessa rolled her eyes. "What will that make me—Mrs. Fifty-eight?"

Only Rodney laughed at her joke. He'd always been a sport.

Nick and Vanessa were properly welcomed with eggnog and cookies, then sent off to their respective beds. For the first night in weeks, Vanessa slept soundly, and visions of sugarplums danced in her head.

When she awakened, her grandmother informed her with glowing eyes that Nick had gone out shopping with Rodney. "He's a fine man," she added, pouring coffee for Vanessa and herself. "You don't need to worry with that one."

Vanessa nodded, her eyes shining as she sat down at the table with Alice. "I love him so much," she said.

Alice's mind had turned to more practical matters. "What about that job in San Francisco?"

"I called and told them I'd changed my mind," she said.

"You're going to stop working then?" Alice asked, trying to be subtle.

Vanessa shook her head, smiling. "I love working. I got in touch with the people at *Seattle This Morning* while I was in town, and we're going into production right after the first of the year."

Alice sighed. "Does that mean there aren't going to be any babies?"

Vanessa patted her grandmother's hand. "There will definitely be babies," she promised. A quick mental calculation indicated that there might be one sooner than anybody expected. She put all the inherent joys and problems of that prospect out of her mind, determined to enjoy Christmas. "Let's go shopping, Gramma. I need to get something for Nick."

The stores were crowded, but Vanessa still enjoyed the displays and the music and the feeling of bustling good cheer. In one shop there were enormous colored balls hanging from proportionate boughs of greenery, and Vanessa felt like a doll standing under a Christmas tree.

She was full of joy when she and Alice arrived home with their packages to find the house crowded with relatives. All of them were gathered around Nick eating take-out chicken and reliving a certain Rose Bowl game.

There was no private time with Nick at all that day, but when Vanessa crept into the living room to put the gifts she'd bought under the tree he was there.

"If you were hoping to catch Santa," he said, turning from the window where he'd been looking out at the steady snowfall, "you're too late. He's already been here."

Vanessa went to Nick and stood on tiptoe to kiss him. "Mistletoe alert," she said, just before her lips touched his.

He laughed and held her very close. "I love you," he said.

Vanessa pretended to pout. "Oh, yeah? Where's my present?" she demanded.

Nick took a small red velvet Christmas stocking trimmed in white fur from a branch of the tree. "Right here," he said.

Vanessa's hand trembled as she pulled a small box from the stocking and looked inside. Nick's gift to her twinkled even in the relative darkness of the living room, and she drew in her breath.

"It's official now," he told her hoarsely. "I'm asking you to marry me, Vanessa. Will you?"

She looked at the ring and then up at Nick and she nodded, her throat too constricted for speech.

He took the ring from its box and slid it on to the proper finger. Christmas magic seemed to shimmer all around them, and it made a sound, too—like wind chimes in a soft breeze. Vanessa hurled her arms around Nick's neck and held on.

Nick stirred a cup of coffee and leaned on the breakfast bar in the kitchen of the house he and Vanessa had bought soon after they were married. His eyes were trained on the television set that hung under one of the cabinets along with the coffee maker and the can opener.

As many times as he'd watched Vanessa do *Seattle This Morning*, he was never bored. If anything, he found her more appealing now that she was obviously pregnant and so, apparently, did her viewers. The ratings were sky-high.

The theme music filled the kitchen and there was Vanessa looking like a shoplifter trying to make off with a basketball. Nick smiled and took a sip of his coffee.

"Good morning, Seattle," she said. "This is Vanessa DeAngelo, and today we're going to talk about..."

Nick heard the buzzer on the drier go off and wandered into the utility room to take his shirts out before they could wrinkle. He put each one on to a hanger and then meandered back into the kitchen. Once Vanessa's show was over, he'd go down to the restaurant, but for now he was a house husband.

He grinned, watching out of the corner of one eye as Vanessa chatted with a group of haggard-looking men. Nick wondered what disaster they'd survived, but he didn't stay to find out. He took the shirts upstairs and hung them in his side of the closet. Then, after peering into the master bath, he shook his head.

As usual, Vanessa had left the place looking like a demilitarized zone. He picked up her towels, hung up her toothbrush and scraped her hairbrush, makeup and other equipment into a drawer.

By the time he got back downstairs, a commercial was on. He was just pouring himself a second cup of coffee when the telephone rang.

"Yo," he said into the receiver, waiting to see what Vanessa's subject for the morning was. She'd told him, but he'd been half asleep and the information had slipped his mind.

"Nick?" The voice belonged to Gina. "I'm calling to remind you about the baby shower. You're supposed to get Vanessa to the restaurant by seven. Can you handle that?"

Nick chuckled, thinking the whole thing sounded like a scene in an espionage novel. "I think so," he said as Vanessa came back on the screen, smiling and telling everybody to stay tuned.

Nick had every intention of doing just that. "Don't worry, Gina," he reassured his sister. "All systems are go."

"Great," Gina said. "What are you doing?"

Terrific. The kid felt sociable. "I'm trying to watch Vanessa's show," he answered pleasantly.

"Oh. Well, goodbye, then."

"See you tonight," Nick responded.

After laying the receiver back in its cradle, he went over to the TV set and turned up the volume slightly.

"Don't you think this is a case of plain and simple hypochondria?" Vanessa was asking of one of her guests.

The man looked, as one of Nick's many aunts liked to say, as if he'd been dragged backward through a knothole. "Absolutely not. If my wife gets a cold, I get a cold. If she stubs her toe, mine hurts."

Nick grinned. The world was full of nut cases.

"When my wife was pregnant," offered the next guest, "I was the one who suffered morning sickness."

Just then, Vanessa was shown in full profile. She was probably going to have twins, Nick thought, and just that morning she'd been a little on the queasy side.

He slapped one hand over his mouth and ran for the bathroom.

New York Times
Bestselling Author

LINDA LAEL MILLER

invites you to experience some

Daring Moves

Amanda Scott had been devastated by a broken love affair. But then
Fate placed handsome widower Jordan Richards right in front of
her...and chemistry took it from there. Was it possible that her life
had just taken a turn for the better?

Just when things are looking up, this new relationship is challenged
by the appearance of her ex-boyfriend. To avoid getting hurt once
again Amanda decides to flee. But first she'll have to answer to
Jordan—and he's not about to let her go without a fight.

In April, find out if true love can mend a broken heart.

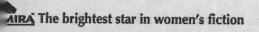

MIRA The brightest star in women's fiction

MLLM5

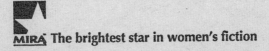

When desires run wild,

Confessions

can be deadly

JoAnn Ross

The shocking murder of a senator's beautiful wife has shaken the town of Whiskey River. Town sheriff Trace Callihan gets more than he bargained for when the victim's estranged sister, Mariah Swann, insists on being involved with the investigation.

As the black sheep of the family returning from Hollywood, Mariah has her heart set on more than just solving her sister's death, and Trace, a former big-city cop, has more on his mind than law and order.

What will transpire when dark secrets and suppressed desires are unearthed by this unlikely pair? Because nothing is as it seems in Whiskey River—and everyone is a suspect.

Look for *Confessions* at your favorite retail outlet this January

MJR

MIRA The brightest star in women's fiction